the size *of the* universe

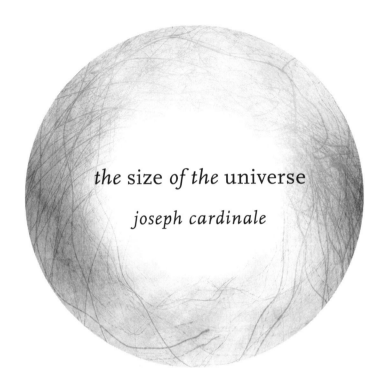

the size *of the* universe

joseph cardinale

FC2

TUSCALOOSA

Copyright © 2010 by Joseph Cardinale
The University of Alabama Press
Tuscaloosa, Alabama 35487-0380
All rights reserved
First edition

Published by FC2, an imprint of The University of Alabama Press,
with support provided by the Publishing Program at the University of
Houston–Victoria.

Address all editorial inquiries to: Fiction Collective Two, University of
Houston–Victoria, School of Arts and Sciences, Victoria, TX 77901-5731

Cover and book design: Lou Robinson
Typefaces: FF Scala and Scala Sans
Produced and printed in the United States of America
∞
The paper on which this book is printed meets the minimum
requirements of American National Standard for Information Sciences—
Permanence of Paper for Printed Library Materials, ANSI Z39.48–1984

Library of Congress Cataloging-in-Publication Data
Cardinale, Joseph.
    The size of the universe / Joseh Cardinale.
        p. cm.
    "Published by FC2, an imprint of the University of Alabama Press,
with support provided by the school of Arts and Sciences, University of
Houston–Victoria."
    ISBN 978-1-57366-158-4 (pbk. : alk. paper)—ISBN 978-1-57366-820-0
(electronic)
    1. Title.
PS3603.A7353S59 2010
813'.6—dc22

                                                        2009047701

for Lisa

Then the man and his wife heard the sound of the LORD God as he was walking in the garden in the cool of the day, and they hid from the LORD God among the trees of the garden. But the LORD God called to the man, "Where are you?"

—Genesis 3:8–9

CONTENTS

ACKNOWLEDGMENTS

Thanks to Noy Holland, Sam Michel, Jason Daniel Schwartz, Alex Phillips, and M. Thomas Gammarino. Greatest thanks to my mother and father. And special thanks to my grandfather, Rocco Porreco, whose writings inspired "Proportions for the Human Figure." Thanks also to the journals in which some of these stories first appeared: "The Singularity" and "Proportions for the Human Figure" in *New York Tyrant*; "Art in Heaven" in *Denver Quarterly*; and "May I Not Seem to Have Lived" in *Web Conjunctions*.

THE SINGULARITY

It began as a game. I was the hider and Sister had to hunt for me. I was not allowed off the field was the first rule, and the second rule was that if I was still hidden at eight o'clock, when Father wanted me to get ready for bed, I would have to come out from wherever I was, the winner. That gave her half an hour of hunting time, minus the five minutes I had to find a hiding place, plus however much extra time we saved if we cleaned the kitchen table and washed the dinner dishes fast enough. I wore a headband and a camouflaged shirt, dark sneakers that she had laced tight for me to run faster if I had to run. I had a wristwatch that counted to the tenths of seconds. I had to hide and hold still watching the seconds turn until the alarm that Sister had set inside the watch went off at eight o'clock or until she found me (she always found me) spread flat in the tall weeds or kneeling in the spider-webbed corner of the bicycle shed or hugging the trunk

1

of a pine tree, trying not to breathe too loudly through a stuffed nose. No matter how often we played this game and no matter where I thought to hide from her, she always found me within five minutes of giving the ready-or-not warning from the porch, and she always spared me a moment, after she shined the flashlight at me, to dash wild and red-faced through the field in screaming laughter, searching out a second and third and sometimes a fourth hiding place before I fell down in the grass defeated and silent and lost. And then she would tag me and walk me back inside the house to help me into my pajamas and tuck me into bed and check for deer ticks in my ears and hair. That was how our games had always gone and that was how this game was about to go tonight if she ever finished washing the dishes. I was going to win this one. I stood behind her in the kitchen, watching her wash and towel the glasses and dishes from the sink and stand them next to one another in the cabinet.

"How many stars are there?" I asked.

"Too many to count," she said.

"I counted them once."

"Did you sponge the table yet?"

"I got to forty-four."

"You can't see every star."

"I could."

"Some of them are too far to see."

"How far?" I asked.

"Infinity," she said. "Clean the table."

I took the sponge from her. I sponged the table clean, pushing the crumbs into my palm and emptying them into the trash bin as she had taught me to do, and then I went back to the sink to see if she was finished with the dishes. I was about to ask her how long infinity would take to walk when the phone rang and she turned the faucet off and dried her hands in time to rush the receiver up on the fourth ring. A friend of hers was on the other end; I knew from how her face lightened and her voice turned higher after she said hello. Her nights lasted longer than mine. Sometimes in bed I would awaken to hear her closing her bedroom door across the hall and turning her radio on high enough for the sound to reach me through the walls, and I could never tell, in those moments how much time still had to pass before the morning would begin again. I listened to her talk to her friend for a while before I opened the back door and told her to come on— we were running out of time. She kept the phone against her shoulder and walked to the door, where she knelt and took my wrist to make sure the alarm in the watch was set to go off. I closed my eyes when she kissed my forehead. When I opened them, she backed up with her palm out and mouthed the words *Ready. Set. Go.*

I knew where to go. Before she shut the door behind me I bounded down the porch steps and through the weeds toward the gigantic maple I had already practiced climbing into when Sister was in her room with her homework that afternoon. It stood high in the center of the field spreading black branches over the grass where just a few days ago I had helped Father turn his sailboat upside down and tarp the bottom for the coming winter. I just had to step on the leaf-covered tarp we tied over the hull to get high enough to reach the lowest branch with both hands. To pull myself with both hands from where I stood on the boat and onto the lowest branch—that was the hardest part I had practiced in the afternoon. That was the part where I had to remember that my body was mine to move where I wanted. I was a living person.

The maple was dying. Sister had said so after one of our games at the beginning of the summer as I lay in the grass under the tree catching my breath for the walk back to bed. She had pointed at the base of a branch where the bark bulged out in the evening light like a balloon grew underneath. *Infected* was a word she used. And then she had noticed round black spots on the leaves fallen out. She had placed her palm on the trunk and bent her neck to see higher as I watched from the grass.

"What do trees do all day?" I asked.

"They grow."

"I never see them grow."

"You have to watch close," she said.

"I am watching," I said. "It's the same size."

Up on the lowest branch I paused against the trunk. I could take two different paths when I planted one foot where the trunk forked and pulled forward. The path I pulled went higher and to the left and higher and to the left until I nested in a snare of stunted branches and orange leaves at the end of a strong limb stretched out over the bottom-up sailboat. Held among the branches and holding still I saw past the trees and the lawn to the light from the kitchen Sister talked on the phone in. I heard her talking.

The second-hand was starting a circle around the wristwatch. At the end of the circle she would have to come for me.

Once I had sleepwalked into her bedroom at night. She remembered for me in the morning. She said she was just about to turn her light off when I walked through her door and sat down at her desk. At the window behind her desk, she said, I watched the wind rain against the glass for a while. Then I had taken her Earth Science textbook from the bookshelf and looked through it until a red leaf she had pressed between two pages drifted out and down to the floor. I let the book go to the floor after the leaf and then pulled open the top drawer of her desk and began picking through the papers and cassettes and coins and notebooks. She walked behind me. "Samuel," she said. She roped her arms around mine so I was stuck. "Calm down." Her grip tightened until she turned me around and asked what I was looking for. I looked at the leaf on the floor.

"The circle," I said.

"What?"

"I can't get out."

"What do you mean?"

"It keeps getting longer."

"Samuel," she said. "Look at me."

"I have to find the circle."

"Look at me, Samuel," she said. "It's not in there."

She looked for me in the eyes. I wasn't there, she said, and so she hugged me for a while and then walked me back to her bed across from the window and set me down on the mattress as she did whenever she tucked me into sleep for the night. Her trick for talking me to sleep was to flatten one palm on my chest and the other over my forehead. And then she would knead her fingers through my hair and tell me to close my eyes and imagine myself floating through outer space. A point of light burned forever ahead of me in the space she told me to imagine floating into.

I watched the second-hand start over on the wristwatch. A bird flew out from the branches behind me.

The porch light turned on. Sister was on the porch sliding the glass door closed behind her with the flashlight in her hand. She stood in her hooded sweatshirt watching the field to see if I would move first or make sound. Her hair was down around her face. Her feet made sounds down the porch steps. A snap of wind shook through the branches and she stopped to lift the hood of her sweatshirt and then knelt in the grass and tied her shoelaces. She called through wind that she was coming for me whether I was ready or not. I held stiller than before.

She walked into the field and pointed the flashlight at the shed slumped above the raspberry bushes. Opening the door of the shed, she sent the light inside, at the rusted shovels and the lawnmower and the bicycles stacked against the walls, and asked if I was in there. I watched her from above. She walked from the shed and past the bushes to the row of pines along the street. To see under the pines she had to stomach down and dust the flashlight along the grass but I wasn't there for her to find this time. I was not in the raked hill of dead leaves she got up to swim her foot through or in the fire-pit squared with concrete blocks. I was not in the weeds she kicked at or the wheelbarrow next to the tomato plants or the hollowed out stump of the elm tree that Father had axed in the autumn our mother died. I was nowhere except the highest branches of the maple watching Sister search the field saying my name. She sat lost below me on the bottom of the sailboat.

"Sam, come out. I'm getting worried."

I looked at the watch. Another four circles and the

alarm would end the game.

I took the watch off and stood silent and still on the limb of the maple. I knew that whatever power I was gathering in that silence would flow out of me and back to her if I told her where I was in the tree. I pitched the watch into the weeds she sat in front of with her face down. She lifted her face to look for the landing sound and, staring at the weeds, said my name like a question.

Nothing answered her. A car was coming down the flat of street I saw from the maple.

She walked against the stiffening wind to the area where the watch had fallen a few steps from the sailboat. I leaned forward against the leaves, feeling the branch I stood on creak and slacken, and watching her troll the light around in the weeds as the car moved closer. She glanced over her shoulder at the shadow of the maple in the grass as if she had an idea. "Are you in the tree?" She moved closer to the tree and shined the light at the leaves under and around the space I was in. "You better not be in there."

The car slowed past the field. It stopped in front of our house and turned into the driveway. Father was home.

"Sam, listen to me. You have to come out right now."

She stared half at the tree and half at the house Father was in front of sooner than we expected him. His door slammed hard. She turned back again and cast the flashlight like a line from a fishing pole into the leaves I held my breath in. She fished around in the branches. A beam of light rivered around me and ran an endless line to the stars.

"Is that you?"

"No," I said.

"Sam, I see you."

"No you don't."

"You little orangutan," she said.

"I want to keep playing."

"How the hell did you get up there?"

"I'm not here," I said. "Go away."

"This is not allowed. You could hurt yourself."

"I can hide anywhere in the field."

"You have to come down from there."

"No," I said. "I'm hiding."

She stood on the sailboat pointing the light straight up at me. Again she told me to come down and again I told her to find me somewhere else. Standing still on the limb with my legs against each other, I felt my arms grow heavier from holding the branch above. I felt the branch I stood on slip at the earth and I was bodiless for a floating moment before I caught the higher one back with both hands and held on.

Something clicked inside the lower branch. Sister screamed her breath in.

"Sam, listen to me," she said. "Do not move."

"You're supposed to tag me."

"It's about to break!"

"I want to keep playing."

"The game is over. We need to get you down right now."

I was fine where I was. The branch underfoot clicked again when I tried to plant more of me on it.

"Stop moving," said Sister. "I told you not to move. It's going to break if you put any more weight down. Just hold on." She had a palm given up over one of her eyes to stop from watching if I was going to fall on her. "Can you go back there?" she asked.

"I don't want to."

"Look over there."

"It's the same thing."

"Look where I'm pointing," she said. She pointed the light where the branch I stood on forked from a harder point at the center of the tree. "Now this is what you're going to do. You're going to pull yourself back toward the trunk, one hand at a time. Slow. You're not going to let go and you're not going to let your feet down. You're going to keep one hand around that branch at all times. You understand?"

I watched the house. Lamplight yellowed the windows of the kitchen. Father walked past the windows on his way upstairs.

"I thought you said not to move."

"You understand me?"

"I can just jump down."

"No. Do not jump."

The light turned on in the upstairs bedroom. I was higher than Father was at the window staring out at the field.

"He's looking for us," I said.

"Don't worry about that now."

"He can't see."

"Can you please just listen to me?"

"We should hide from him."

"Don't worry about that now."

"I'm not."

"Go toward the trunk then."

I was older than she thought. I looked at the window again and started laughing and at that instant the alarm went off inside the watch I had thrown away. Sister turned from me fast to see what the sound was coming from in the weeds, shielding the light ahead of her as if to catch a wild animal in the act of pouncing. Nothing was still there. A squirrel hurried across the grass. The alarm beeped a few times before she circled the light back to me in the tree. I was still laughing at something.

"I'm over there," I said.

"No you're not."

"I'm in the watch."

"Sam," she said.

"I'm not Sam."

In the morning after I sleepwalked into her bedroom I had slept late. I remember thrashing up from the bottom of a falling dream and finding her room full of sunlight from the window over her desk. Her window was open and I remember noticing first her Earth Science textbook opened flat on the floor and second the sound of water running in the bathroom down the hall from her open door. A mess of papers and photos and odds of trash seemed to have tided out from the half-open drawer of her desk and fallen down to the floor in the breeze that cooled through the screens and shook the wind-chimes hanging over the window. I heard the water stop running in the bathroom. I heard her footsteps down the hall until she was in the room with me. A white towel was coiled tight around her wet hair. She asked if I remembered how I had gotten here and I said I last remembered falling asleep in my bed. As she told the story of how I had sleepwalked into her bedroom, I stared at a photograph of me in the field from three years ago that she had framed on her desk next to the radio. I didn't believe her. "That wasn't me," I said when she stopped talking, and she looked at me as if I were far away.

"It wasn't," I repeated.

"Then who was it?"

"I don't know," I said.

"You don't *remember*."

"It changes."

"What does?"

"I can't see it."

"You can't remember it."

"I sleep in my bed."

"You fell asleep there."

"That's where I sleep."

"Yes. And you walked here."

"No," I said. "I don't remember doing that."

It was hard for me then to make her understand. That the body I was in had sleepwalked to her room in the night I believed, even if I remembered nothing of what she had told me. In the same way I believed I was once the child in the photograph on her desk. And yet the body that sleepwalked to her room in the night was not the same as the one that woke in her bed in the morning or stood for the photograph in the field. It was not the same body that held still in the tree now watching her point the flashlight up and listening to the alarm beep on from the weeds. No line connected one instance of that body to the next except the words that I remembered and the name that she called at me from the grass. And that was nothing. That was what I would have told her in the morning if I had found the words and that was what I was laughing at now as I watched her from the branch of the maple. That even if I brought the body I was right now down to the earth she would never find me. I was already dead.

"I'm nothing," I said.

"Sam," she said.

"I'm not Sam."

"Yes you are."

"It's all the same."

"Take another step. You're almost there."

"It's all a dream," I said. "We're dreaming this."

In the long instant after I spoke those words and before I fell from the tree, I stood still in the light she shined at me, seeing her speak but no longer hearing what she was telling me to do. I heard instead the alarm speeding on, speeding faster and becoming louder each time, as if wanting her to rescue it from the weeds before she rescued me from the tree. A space of silence followed each beep, I noticed, and each beep sounded the same as the one before and the one after. I had never noticed that sameness or that space of in-between silence before. Since she always found me in time to switch the alarm off after a few seconds, I had never heard the beeping go on for so long and so far. I let go of the branch above as I listened to the alarm. I saw above me the line of light from the flashlight lengthening past the leaves at the stars that she had told me were too many to count. And when the branch broke under me, when I broke the branch downward and began falling with my body at a certain speed toward the earth she stood on, falling forward, so that the head was going to hit first, I heard the alarm not as a sequence of separate beeps repeated over and over again, but as a single unbroken line of sound that seemed to go on as long as the light of the stars, still moving through each instant of time I fell through. I saw the bottom of the sailboat coming up at me fast.

But I did not hit the sailboat. What hit the sailboat was the head in which I had fallen and the body that fell after the head and crumpled into the grass. In the instant after that body deadened still next to where Sister stood screaming the word *no*, I saw a starless darkness I could not awaken from. How deep that darkness was and how long I was inside of it I didn't know. I felt nothing where the feeling should have been of bones and broken skin. Still I heard from somewhere afar the sound of the alarm flat-lining across the blackness and rushing onward before breaking again into separate beeps. A pinprick of white light appeared far ahead of me, blinking in and out along with the beat of the alarm, and growing larger and closer with each blink. When the light reached me, when I reached the light, I saw for a time Sister's face leaned over me open-mouthed, still as a photograph, weeping for me to wake up. Then the stillness broke and I lifted out of the eyes that saw her, through her weeping face and toward the branches of the tree I had fallen from, past the branches and into the night overhead, watching her as I rose higher.

Sam was not moving. I saw his body still where she held him in her lap. I saw a light fogged around her, glowing from a sun inside her, so bright that the crisscrossed branches seemed see-through as glass under me as I floated higher over the tree. I saw the roots of the tree going into the ground like glowing wires and mixing into the roots of the other trees in the field. I saw blood pooled on the sailboat where Sam had hit and I saw Father opening the door and calling our names. I saw how she held Sam as if he were sleeping, his head cradled closed-eyed in her elbow, his face bleeding onto her arms and his legs bent and hanging down like stumps over her lap and into the weeds. I saw into her thoughts as she held him and I saw into her feelings and into her future. I saw that she was thinking that he was dead and that she was alive and that she felt nothing still in her. She was never going to feel like Sister again.

Her light grew dimmer as I lifted farther from the land. It was as if the sun inside her was flaring out and falling into itself, pulling inward the light from the houses around her and the heavens above and leaving the face of earth darker than before. And I thought as I watched her disappear inside that darkness that I might go back to the dead body she held if I tried to. I think still that if I had let go of whatever was lifting me at that moment I might have fallen back to life and awakened as Sam again in her arms. I did not want to, though. I was too enormous to fit into that little body she held in her lap. I held still instead to what lifted me where I was going deeper into the growing dark. I found that I went faster when I held stiller and that the faster I went the less of earth I saw and the more of space and time I seemed to take on and hold inside. I was a single point growing bigger and lighter and longer like a balloon spreading out past the stars to the ends of the infinite universe. It was all becoming the same.

THE GREAT DISAPPOINTMENT

After the flood began I was alone with Mother in the house from before. Neither of us knew what to do. We lived in a watchtower house at the peak of the mountain—of what was once the mountain—and after the last big wave came up, the lower half was underwater and the waves were splashing up at the top floor. We waited upstairs. There was nothing else to do. In the night we slept badly because it rained often and hard and we were afraid of turning over and falling dead in our sleep. Her bunk was below mine. A long window was square on the wall across from our beds and all night the rain came down and I lay waking and waiting to wake up again in a dream about drowning. Perhaps I never dreamt. Before dawn the rain would stop and the wind would slow down and after she had come out from her blankets she would look through the window at the water and announce that the sun was out, the sun was out. The sun was always out in the morning, on that part of the planet. In the evening the gray clouds would gather over us again and the sky would blacken and whatever of the sea had evaporated in the warmth of the day would come back down in the starless cool of the night.

In the days she went out to the roof of the porch with her fishing pole. She fished. I followed her out and sat on the windowsill watching for help. Inside the water in every direction swam bluefish and fluke and other creatures that she lifted sometimes with her fishing pole and placed in the bucket for us to eat when we were hungry. Sometimes we thought we saw visions of the Savior walking on the water: a robed figure slumped forward and stumbling across the calm surface as if he were learning how to walk upright, his arms hanging so low that his fingers seemed to skim the water for balance. Always he would sink under again before I knew for sure what to call him. She seemed to know somehow that he was coming to save us.

"I'm leaving," I sometimes said.

"No you're not."

"I am."

"Okay," she said. "Where are you going?"

"Somewhere else," I said.

"You are somewhere else."

Once she had drawn a real-looking picture of the Savior walking on the water. In the drawing, which she taped on the wall of our bedroom, he was very dark and very far away. He was just the shadow of something shaped like a person slouched upright and leaning forward as he walked. There was no way of concluding that this shadow was the walking Christ, much less that Christ was coming to save us from the flood. But nor was there any way of concluding otherwise. I looked at the drawing often in the minutes after Mother went outside to fish and what I always ended up wishing was that I could somehow erase him from the rest of it. He distracted me. He seemed to demand more attention than he deserved. Sometimes sitting up from bed I would place my thumb over him—that was how small he was—and I would try to forget he was there. *The Second Coming,* said the caption that Mother had printed in dark letters at the bottom of the picture.

So much time must have passed. I saw him so often that I grew used to the disappointment I felt when he vanished and yet rarely enough that each new sighting incited a certain hope that he was almost here—whatever he was. And yet predicting when he was going to appear or where or for how long he would walk before us before he was gone again was impossible. Sometimes we saw him several times on the same day and sometimes he would seem to go months without coming up once.

"Maybe he's just a fish," I said.

"Fishes aren't shaped like that."

"They could be."

"He's the same every time."

"So is everything else."

"He's not a fish."

"I'm just saying we don't know," I said.

After a while she decided to start keeping track of him. I was the recorder. In the pages of a notebook I wrote down columned lists documenting when he appeared and where and how long the sight of him seemed to last before he disappeared. I just wrote what she said to write: time, duration, location. She said if we recorded the facts carefully and if we looked at the lists of facts together and from the right angle then at some point a pattern would come into shape and show us what the Savior was thinking. He wanted us to figure out the pattern for ourselves before he saved us.

I wanted to believe her. In another notebook I began converting the list of sightings into graphs and graphing each entry along a grid that stood for the sea. At the center where the X and Y axes crossed I drew a circle representing our house and around this circle I drew small points to mark each of the places we seemed to see the Savior walking on the water. To fit them all on the same page I had to keep erasing the points and making the spaces between them longer and shorter depending what she said she remembered. If she remembered wrong sometimes, I never said too much.

"How do you know?" I asked her once.

"How do I know what?"

"That we're doing this right."

"That there's a pattern?"

"Even if there is a pattern," I said.

"We're supposed to look for it."

"But how do you know we're getting the facts right?"

"What do you mean, *right*?"

"I mean do you have any proof?"

"No one has proof."

"That's what I mean."

"Of anything," she said.

"That's what I'm saying."

"Right," she said. "So we're looking for it."

I studied the list of sightings, but I never quite believed in them. At her request I made up a system of signifying the duration of each sighting through the size and shade of the points on the graph. A bigger and darker point meant that the Savior had remained visible on the water long enough for us to call for him from the roof before he vanished under—a rare occurrence. More common were the small faint dots marking sudden visions that seemed to start and stop at the exact same instant. But knowing where to draw the dots and how dark to make them got harder and harder as time passed. Too many new dots were there to count and keep track of the old ones. If I had a clock to time each sighting and the time to measure out each point and test the lengths between them, I might have been able to believe in what I was doing. Since she was never satisfied that I had gotten the shades right I ended up having to draft a new graph every few days, tracing over the day before's and lightening or darkening the points she told me to. Telling her that this wasn't going to work would have taken too long. I watched the water and graphed the facts.

Nothing much changed. No matter how many nights passed, the sun seemed forever to start from the same place on the horizon ahead and path the same blue arc across the heavens before setting under against the other side. And every night after the rains began and we moved from the roof to our room she would clean the room up and light candles and spread the day's graph on the table to see if she could see the pattern taking shape in the points I had drawn. I laddered up to the top bunk and took the flashlight from the shelf and steadied the glow from the bulb still on the page to help her see. At first she'd walk in circles around the table with a pencil in her hand, sometimes angling her head to see the graph from different sides and sometimes stopping for a long time to kneel on the floor and flatten her forehead against the page like she was praying or peering through the eyepiece of a microscope at a single point. Holes, she said once when I asked her what she was looking for. Another time she said she was looking for the face of God. Finished looking, she would set to drawing connecting lines between different points on the graph, straight and diagonal, making shapes like the constellations we used to see when the nights were clear. But the constellations she drew were different every night and none of them spelled out the pattern she wanted to see.

"It's not here yet," she said.

I was running out of blank pages to start over with. As time passed so many points were added to each new graph that the lengths between them disappeared and she needed to use a magnifying glass to distinguish one from another. Soon the entire page was covered not in separate points but in pointed shades of gray that grew out darker and darker from the white circle of our home in the center and then whitened again at each of the four corners. From a distance the graphs were starting to look like wide open eyeballs watching back.

"I can't do this anymore," I said.

"You're not doing anything."

"I'm trying. It's not working."

"That's the point."

"Still," I said.

"That's how we grow."

"I know. But I feel like we're getting smaller. You know?"

She fished from the roof. I sat on the windowsill watching from the water and back to the graph that represented the water. In real life I was remembering that the circle in the center of the graph was still where our house was— that we were still right here. But looking too long at the circle felt like spinning down to the bottom of a funnel: faster, faster. I had to stop before I fell out the other side.

"We're the same size," she said.

"Compared to each *other* we are."

"You've grown a little taller, in fact."

"That's not what I mean."

"Okay," she said. "You don't mean our bodies."

"No. I mean not *just* that."

"What, you mean our souls?"

"No," I said. "I mean everything."

"Everything we are?"

"And everything we aren't. You know?"

"Sure," she said. "But compared to what?"

She looked at me as if she was just asking. Then she turned back and cast the line out from the end of the pole in her hands to the water.

I would have said something else if I wasn't starting to feel sick of it inside. That everything inside and out was getting smaller compared to something forever else: some permanently still turning point that was never going to grow longer or shorter or higher or lower or lighter or darker. I couldn't get closer to it. A coiled feeling was spinning out of me from the stomach. A fish was pulling down at the hook beneath the water—hardening the fishing line flat from the pole she held bent with her back to me on the roof. If she was reeling the fish up from the water I was supposed to bring the bucket over to her and help her take the hook out. I sat back down on the windowsill before I could stand. "I feel sick," I said. Then I was leaning down with my arms around the bucket she had brought for me instead of the fish. She was kneeling in front of me with her hand on the back of my head, telling me to breathe in and out. Just breathe. Nothing came out when I thought I was throwing up.

"You should lie down," she said. "Can you stand up?"

"I can't do this anymore."

"Your head is burning."

"I'm fine. I need something to drink."

"Come on. I'll get you some water."

"Cold," I said. "Did you catch the fish?"

"Fluke," she turned around. "Small. See?"

I leaned back against the window to look where she was looking. At the edge of the roof a fluke was spread flat as land and pulsing to death in the morning sun. "I can't eat that," I said. "I am not going to eat that." A long feeling passed through me. She walked to the fluke and pulled the hook out from its face. She was lifting it still breathing in her hands to put in the bucket of water when I stood and climbed through the window to lie back down. I climbed to the top bunk and stared up at the picture.

Before I fell asleep I tried to see back to what our lives had been like before the flood. In flashes I saw evening forests and the figures of others shaped like us watching from high in the branches and moving from one branch to another as I walked a worn path through the trees.

It was almost morning again when I woke up. I sat up and saw her sitting candlelit at the table with her fist to her chin and four identical-looking graphs spread out before her. In a white bowl at the corner of the table were the bones of the fluke she had taken living from the water a few hours ago. She tapped the point of her pencil twice against one of the graphs and began darkening a spot in the top-right quadrant.

I took the flashlight from the shelf on the wall and shined the light on her until she lifted her eyes at me. She asked me if I felt better.

"A little," I said. "I don't know. I feel tired."

"You slept for sixteen hours."

"I have a headache."

"I've been up all night looking at these graphs."

"It's behind my eye."

"You were talking in your sleep."

"It keeps starting and stopping."

"You're dehydrated."

"That smell," I said.

"Drink some water."

"Can you throw that fish out?"

I drank from the glass of water she had left on the shelf behind me. She opened the window and left the remains of the fluke out on the roof.

"Sun's coming up," she said.

She was in her morning mood, singing to herself as she sat back down at the table and studied the graphs. Now and then she asked without looking at me if I was going to get out of bed or if I wanted to eat. I wasn't answering. I was thinking about where I was going to go if I left. After a while I stopped thinking and started listening to her turning through the pages of her notebook and talking to me—she must have been talking for a few minutes now—about the patterns she was seeing in the points I had drawn before I was sick. She thought she was on to something this time. She had looked through the last three graphs, she said, and figured it out. In the past three weeks we had seen the Savior surface in a total of ten different locations at ten different times. If we added up the coordinates of each of those ten locations and split the sum in half, and if we then multiplied *that* number by three—one for each spatial dimension—we arrived at the number one-thousand-two-hundred-and-thirty-four. Add the digits up and start over from there: $1 + 2 + 3 + 4$. That gives us 10, and since that's the same number we started with, we know that we're getting somewhere and that we're stuck between one and zero.

She sat at the table writing lines in her notebook as she talked. I asked her what she was talking about and she handed me a page filled with numbers and letters and squares and equal signs. Her pencil pointed to an equation written at the center: $MV(2) / 2 - GMg / r = 0$. A circle was drawn around it.

"Does that mean anything to you?" she asked.

"I'm not doing this anymore."

"You said part of it in your sleep."

"That? No I didn't."

"You did. You kept saying *gamma*."

"And that's how you got the equation?"

"Just that GM part," she said.

"I'm not doing this anymore."

"The rest is from the graphs."

"And what does the rest of it mean?"

"I don't know," she said. "But I think it means he's coming today."

I turned back inside the blankets. As she readied for the day, taking the fishing pole and the bucket and bait from the closet and going over her graphs again, I sat in the bed looking at the picture of the Savior on the wall above me. In the picture the sun was a half-circle permanently in the midst of rising over the horizon or setting under it. I wasn't sure which. Staring at the picture I remembered what she had once said long ago when I asked her where the sun went at night. She had said that it went underwater—that God put the sun out so we could sleep and then placed a new one in the sky in the morning. Every sun, she said, is completely different from the one you saw yesterday. We were standing on the roof, that day, skipping flat stones across the flatter waves, and she was telling me that the stones were our thoughts and that the water was God. It all goes under. There was truth there. Not enough. I looked at the sun—the one in the picture. I did not think. I just looked and looking thought what I saw. *Water*, I thought. *Water*, I thought, and in time the repetition of this word seemed to remind me where I was—to stop the feeling of falling out of my eyes and into the picture. I was still in the house. I wasn't going anywhere. I leaned back in the bed and held my hands over my face and shut my eyes all the way down.

"Hey," she said. "You feel okay?"

"No. I don't know."

"What are you doing?"

"Dreaming," I said.

"No you're not."

"I'm trying to."

"You see anything?"

"Not yet," I said.

"Then open your eyes."

"I can't. Can you leave me alone a minute?"

She went out to the roof. I lay in bed in the room of the house and I tried to forget where I was.

Behind my eyes was a squared and still and absolutely depthless darkness. I was in the darkness and falling down and at the same time outside of it and watching up through a fallen screen. I felt the whole black world inside me ballooning out and out and out and taking on everything behind and in front of me. No light entered. No sound could be heard. I thought at first that if I kept my eyes shut and thought hard enough I might pilot that square of darkness like a spaceship out of my head and out to the edges of whatever I was, but I found—I always found—that I couldn't get out from inside the locked space inside my skull, where the words were telling me who I had been and where I was now and what I was about to do next. I was here in the house. I heard the wind start and the line go out from her fishing pole. Listening closer I heard her singing a psalm to herself as she sometimes did. Her cup runneth over. Surely goodness and mercy shall follow her all the days of her life. I waited for the last line, which she always delivered like a threat, as if she were talking down at the clouds from the top of the mountain. *And I will dwell in the house of the Lord forever!* Whether you want me or not, was what she seemed to mean. But no: for some reason she was no longer singing.

A long time passed without me. I kept my eyes closed and listened for her through all the little creaking sounds of the house. Through the sounds of the water slapping up I heard a sudden sharp splash, like a stone thrown hard and hitting the calm surface, and then an instant after that came her pleading voice screaming a single word that sounded like either *no* or *now*—and then there a was flat thump and a sudden rush of wind through the open window that shook the walls for a few short seconds.

After that all was still again. In the stillness I heard the long whining sound of something like a human animal coming from out on the roof. I sat up open-eyed, as if from a falling dream, and looked around the room at the graphs drifted all over the floor. Hours had passed since she went outside. I saw from the afternoon shadows. Out the window I couldn't see her from the top bunk, but I still heard the low whining of whatever it was she had pulled from the sea getting louder and softer. Then I heard her calling for me. Her voice was slow and strangely distant, as if she didn't want to wake me up.

I lifted out from the blankets and took a few long breaths before I leapt down from the bunk. It had been so long since I last stood up that I fell over on my knees as soon as I touched the floor. A glass of water was eyelevel on the table. I sat for a moment drinking the water and then stood and walked to the window. Her eyes didn't lift up at me when I looked out. She was standing at the end of the roof facing the house and looking down.

A long animal was under her.

At first I saw only that the animal wasn't moving. Then I saw that it wasn't going to move.

It was still breathing. It was shaped like a star or a person. Its arms were open and spread out crosswise so that one hand hung off the edge of the roof and the other was at her feet.

I was starting to understand. I shut my eyes and opened them and everything was still the same.

"What is that?" I asked.

"I told you he was coming."

"You caught him?"

"Go get him some water."

He was the Savior. I knew that more the less I thought. But he looked nothing like the visions we had seen and nothing like the figure in the picture that Mother had drawn. In the picture he might have passed for an angel. Now I saw that he was something more like an underwater ape. He was coated in thick reddish hair except for his face and hands and feet. His arms were longer than his legs. His closed eyes were set deep and his face was flat and bowled out at the mouth. In his cheek was the hook from the fishing pole. He was chewing his mouth open and closed, open and closed, and then he lifted his hand and grasped at the hook without getting hold of it. I looked at Mother. She circled around him like a huntress, watching him with one thought at a time. She would have to throw him back, I thought, and then I thought again. He was here to save us. He was dying. "Do something," she said.

"I don't understand."

"It was an accident."

"You fished him out?"

"He's light."

"He's not a fish."

"I reeled him in. He's lighter than he looks."

"He looks like a tree creature," I said.

"He's not a creature."

"I think he's dying."

"So *do* something," she said. She went through the window when I got out of the way. I followed her through the bedroom and out the door and down the hall to the bathroom to get the bandages and water from the closet. She washed her hands in the sink, watching me in the mirror until I laughed and looked at the floor. "I told you he was coming today," she said. She dried her hands on her shirt and went outside—I went after her—and walked to where the Savior would see us. But his eyes were still closed. He was inside his face.

She sat down next to him and felt for the pulse in his neck. "This might hurt," she said. One of her hands was on his chest and with the other she pried his mouth open and pulled the hook out from inside. He opened his eyes suddenly and looked around and around the roof without seeming to figure out where he was. His eyes were small and dark—too dark to see into—and he didn't seem to see what he was looking at. I saw nothing human in his eyes. No light. I felt I was looking into the eyes of a bug.

"I think he's blind," I said.

He leaned back down and closed his eyes again. He hardly moved. For a long time Mother worked over him, cleaning up the blood around his mouth, pouring water over his face, picking out seashells and snails and algae from his arms and legs. She held her palm on his forehead for a while and said again and again that he was all right. He was going to be all right.

He opened his eyes and looked back and forth from her to the water a few times as if for some connection between here and there. And then he closed his eyes and twitched a few times as if electrocuted. After that he was absolutely still. She leaned her ear to his chest.

"He's fine," she said. "I think he's just in shock."

She stood and sat next to me on the windowsill with her arms crossed and for several minutes we watched him sleep. His chest rose and fell with each breath. Sometimes an awful and unintelligible sound would seem to originate from him—something like the moan of an animal lost and lingering in the place where the master was last seen.

"What's he saying?"

"I don't know."

"Eiuhwla," he said.

"Do you understand that?"

"No," she said.

"We can't understand you," I said.

"Don't talk to him like that."

"Aueiylhiee," he said.

"What does that mean?"

"Did you hear me," she said. "Stop it."

Nothing was about to happen. I watched from the windowsill. After a while his presence on the roof began to seem as normal as that of the seagull watching us from the gutter or the clouds of flees orbiting around his sleeping face. "I guess we should bring him inside," she said. "Put him in the attic." I took hold of his legs when she asked me to. She took his arms and we carried him down inside the house and up the stairs to the attic. I'd thought that carrying him up there would take a lot of energy, but he was much lighter than he appeared. At one point as we went up the stairs his foot grasped at me like a hand, and when I let go of him, he hovered as if underwater and remained in the air long enough for me to catch him back up. I was faster than I thought. We set him down on his back in the center of the rug beside the attic window overlooking the porch we fished from. Pushed against the wall of the attic where the ceiling sloped down were cardboard boxes full of books, canned food, and clothes we had brought upstairs when the basement began to flood. I pulled the string that used to turn on the big light bulb that hung from the ceiling.

"So what do we do now?" I asked.

"Sit down. Wait for him to wake up."

"How long is he going to sleep?"

"I don't know."

"I thought he was supposed to be God."

"He is. He's inside that body right now."

"Then why doesn't he come out?"

"I don't know," she said. "Just sit down."

I sat on the sofa waiting for him to do something else. He paid no attention to the bowl of rainwater she filled from a glass pitcher and placed on the floor beside him. When she knelt and pushed the bowl closer to him he got on his stomach and licked at the water a few times and then let his face fall into the bowl. For a second I feared he might drown. A few bubbles rose to the surface of the water before she pulled his head out of the bowl—she pulled him by his neck-hair—and pushed him over on his back again so he could breathe easier. "He might be hungry," she said. "I should get him something to eat." She told me to watch him closely and call her back upstairs if he did anything. I sat on the sofa.

Alone with him I began to lose interest. Remembering that he was the Savior or that I was perhaps in the presence of God did nothing for me. He slept too much, whatever he was. I looked out the window at the roof of the porch. Mother took a bluefish she had caught that morning out from the bucket of water. She slapped the face of the bluefish two hard times against the roof. I went to look through the boxes of old books stacked against the wall. A book about animals was at the top. I sat down with the book and leafed through the pictures of the great apes to see which one looked most like the Savior on the floor. In one picture an orangutan was swinging between the branches of two trees and about to let go of one of them. He was thinking several trees ahead.

She was coming up the stairs. In her hands when she elbowed open the door was a plateful of fresh bluefish that she set on the floor in front of his face. He slept, slept. If what she said was true he would wake up soon and eat the fish and do what he was supposed to do. His flesh hungered even if the inside was God space. Sleeping and eating would strengthen him to save us and whatever else had survived the flood. After that the saints and angels would resurrect and rule the earth with him for one thousand years. We would live among the last of the physical people and ascend to heaven at the end of his reign. I watched him from the sofa. She was better than I was at watching, perhaps because she was older than I was and more accustomed to time. I was thinking hours into the future. In the future I would have to lie down in bed and go to sleep again. Shadows were growing from the attic corners to the clean circle of sunlight he slept in. Watching him was getting harder. After a while I went back to reading the book on my lap. At night orangutans sleep in nests pulled back from the branches of trees. I was at the word *cling* when Mother asked what I was looking at. I pointed at the picture of the orangutan.

"I think that's him," I said.

"That's an orangutan."

"It looks like him."

"That's not him."

"But he's like that."

"That's just the form he took."

"Yeah," I said, "but why an orangutan?"

"He can take all different forms."

"But I'm asking why he took this form. Of all the forms—"

"I don't know," she said. "Just put the book away. Pay attention."

I tried. She reminded me often when I lost faith how fortunate I was to witness the end of the world. So many generations had been disappointed. A long time ago a mathematician named William Miller had calculated that the Savior would return sometime on a certain night the following year. Miller had convinced several thousand believers to abandon their coastal homes and follow him to the burned-over clearing in the center of the island where the Savior was expected to descend from the heavens in a chariot of flames. On the appointed date the faithful had camped in the center of the clearing and watched the sun move from morning to night. Nothing happened. When midnight passed the crowd grew restless and began returning to their homes and eventually to older churches. But Miller alone remained in the clearing, kneeling in the place where the lord's chariot failed to land, his head bowed, according to the stories, and ablaze with a benign anger at the heavens. He remained for three days, meditating. In his mind he made up a new religion based on the belief that the Savior had indeed returned at the prophesied hour and taken the form of a wild animal born somewhere in the surrounding forest. Miller had gone into the forest alone to hunt for the Christ animal.

It was almost dark. She leaned forward at the floor with her elbow on her knee and her head rested against her open palm. I asked her if she was awake. Her eyes opened and she stood from the sofa and paced two circles around the Savior's body. Watching him, she picked up a matchbook and lit the candle on the end table and blew the match out. "This house is too long," she said. She looked along the walls, her hand rubbing the side of her head, and then she sat down on the chair across from me. For a few seconds she sat staring at me as if she had forgotten who I was and what I was doing here. I was starting to forget too. And then her face calmed back open and I recognized her again as the one who knew what to do next. "Come on," she said. "Let's go back downstairs." I followed her to the door, but then she turned around and went back to check on the Savior one more time. Her palm touched his face. She picked up the blanket from the arm of the sofa and flagged it over him. When she blew the candle out everything seemed a lot darker than it had a minute ago.

"Turn the flashlight on," she said.

"I don't have it."

"Yes you do."

"No, it's on the table."

I watched her shape moving around in the dark. Then the flashlight turned on, making a circle of light on the wall.

She walked to the door with the light in front of her. I followed her down the stairs. In the bedroom I climbed to the top bunk where she gave me the flashlight and lifted the covers over me like the nights before. She asked me if I was hungry. I said I wasn't eating anymore—I was fasting. I shined the flashlight on the picture of the Savior walking on water as she moved through the room lighting candles and cleaning up for the morning. In the corner of the picture she had drawn a cloud that looked to me like the face of someone I used to know. But I doubted I'd ever known anyone else.

It was starting to rain. I turned the flashlight off. I listened to her fall into the bottom bunk and flip through the pages of the graphs as the rain hardened in the wind around the house. Then she dropped the graphs on the floor and blew the candle out.

At this point on every other night she would clasp her hands and commence praying out loud. In her prayers she always asked for an end to our waiting. She asked the Lord to rend the heavens and come down to earth so that the sea would boil and the mountains tremble before him. But now that the Lord was in our attic there was nothing to ask for.

"You feel all right?" I asked.

"I don't know what to do."

"You want to talk?"

"Sure. I don't know."

"Tell me a story."

"I don't know any more."

"Tell the one about William Miller."

"You know that one."

"I can't remember the end."

"He goes into the forest."

"Then what happens?"

She said nothing. I lay on my side watching the window. It was as dark as the wall.

And then I saw a flash of lightning that framed for an instant the rain falling above the sea. I saw in that light that each particular raindrop was disappointed because the fall was about to end forever. In the sea everything was stuck together. I was having trouble breathing. I breathed through my nose in the *one-two-three* rhythm she had taught me to remember when I felt I was drowning. She had taught me to pull each breath to the bottom of my stomach and then push the air all the way out of time.

"I know what you are," she said.

"You're still awake?"

"That's how I felt. Faces."

"Okay," I said. "What am I?"

There was a silence. And then there was a long drag of thunder from outside the window.

"Wait," she said. "What did I just say?"

"You said you know what I am."

"Faces," she said. "I know."

"You're not making sense."

"You're sixteen years old."

"Seventeen," I said. "So?"

"I used to feel like that."

"I don't feel like anything."

"You do. You feel like other people."

"You should go back to sleep."

"Like there's no difference."

"No difference between what?"

She didn't answer. I lay in bed staring up at the dark and listening to the breathing sounds.

In a dream I was flat on the seafloor. A fluke splashed through the water as if dropped from the sky and spiraled down at me like a leaf. I swam past the fluke toward the circle of sunlight on the other side. Before I surfaced, I looked back for the fluke floating down from me in the dream. I wanted to see if it was still alive. But instead of the fluke in the water I saw the Savior rising from the floor of the attic. His blanket fell as he stood to look out the window. He was looking for a tree to make a nest in.

I sweated awake in the dark. In bed I listened for a while to the Savior restlessly pacing the attic. I could tell from his footsteps that he was lost. He couldn't remember how he had gotten here. He walked back and forth through the attic until something fell on the floor sounding like him—as if he had fallen over on his face and was facing down at me through the floor. Then I heard him whining again as he had on the roof. He whined for a long time and sometimes I let up listening to him and listened rather to the rain and wondered if the rain was still there even when I forgot about it. Then I forgot again about the rain and wondered what he was whining about.

I had to save him. Folding my legs over the side of the bed, I took the flashlight from the shelf behind me and shined the light on the floor and leapt down into it.

I landed and pointed the light at her. She slept facing the wall. I followed the light out of our room and through the hall up the stairs. At the attic door I began to think again. I wasn't sure what had brought me there. I was trying to recall something I had known when I walked up the stairs—some sequence of sounds or words that had repeated inside me from the time I decided to save him. But the sound grew farther away from me the harder I listened for it. I remembered a morning on the roof when I watched her flatten on her stomach and lower the back of her hand into the water. She made a fist in the instant before a fish swam over her open palm.

I stood still as her hand in the water at the door he was behind. I knocked once and nothing answered me. After another few knocks I heard the sound of the chair falling down.

I remembered her telling me that after he went into the forest, William Miller had searched for years without finding the Christ animal. He had recorded his movements during these years in a four-hundred page journal that was discovered in his abandoned tent after his death. In his journal Miller catalogued every animal he caught sight of during his endless walks. He drew no clear line between one animal and the next. He thought of each as a potential incarnation of Christ. He believed that the Christ animal longed for recognition and would reveal his divinity to humanity the moment he was addressed by his true name. And so to every moving creature Miller encountered in the wilderness he shouted the name of God. *I know what you are,* he exclaimed after each shout. Most of the animals ran from him, though, and the few bold enough to hold their ground answered him in languages he made no sense of.

I turned the knob and pushed the door open. What I saw in the attic was the Savior lifting his face from the plate on the floor and looking into the light from the flashlight that I had forgotten in my hand. He did not move—not for a long time. He looked less afraid than ashamed to have been caught in the act of eating on his stomach in a strange house. I was ashamed to have caught him. I pointed the flashlight away from his eyes and at the plate of fish as though that was what I had come for—to look at the fish. Nothing remained on the plate except the head and some bones and scales of flesh. He licked at the scraps without taking his eyes away from the light for longer than a second or two. Finished eating he pushed the plate away and leaned forward on his long forearms with his legs spread behind him and his head aloft and proud as if waiting for an answer. I was waiting for the question.

He said nothing. His eyes revealed nothing more than passing interest in me as long as I kept the flashlight still. As if from another world he stared and stared at the light for a long time without seeming to find what he was looking for—and yet still looking. Then he arched his back and began to approach me. I thought of the word *no*. In the moment after that word I knew somehow what he wanted me to do. He wanted me to guide him back home. I held the flashlight up and started backing up from the attic and down the stairs, calling for him to come after me. He followed at a few steps distance, watching the circle. At the top of the staircase he stopped and stared down at the light for a long time before he set his hand down on the first step. He wasn't used to stairs. He took one step at a time and rested for a moment on each to make sure he was still there. I stood at the bottom of the staircase shining the light up.

When he was at the second-to-last step I left him and went ahead to the bedroom to make sure Mother was sleeping. Even when she slept I saw some space between her eyelids. She never fully shut them.

I heard him walking down the hall. He seemed to know not to make too much noise. He was just coming through the door when I pushed the window open and climbed outside to the roof.

The rain was lighter and warmer than it sounded from inside. I thought for a second about leaping into the water. Instead I pointed the flashlight through the open window and saw the Savior hunched over the graphs on the floor next to her bed. He leaned over the graphs in the same posture as he had leaned over the bowl of fish in the attic, as if sniffing at them, and whined. Then he went over to her bed and watched her sleep. If she was awake she might have warned me to leave him alone—to trust him.

I didn't. In the last pages of his journal, I remembered, Miller had discovered a new strategy for searching for Christ. His strategy was to stop searching, to remain where he was in the forest and wait for God to find him. His mistake, he decided, was to believe that he had to hunt for the Savior, when in fact the Savior was hunting for *him* and would only appear in the moment his mind grew still and silent as the stars. He resolved at that point to set a campfire outside his tent and to sit in front of the fire pronouncing the name of God and nothing else over and over again until he died. *Let us then go backward,* he wrote on the final page of his journal. *It is death to go forward; to go backward can be no more.* That was the last thought Miller recorded before his mauled remains were found beside his tent at the edge of the forest, embers still smoking in the bed of his stone-encircled campfire. He was less than two miles from the place where our house stood now in the falling rain.

I shined the flashlight down through the window at the wall. He turned and looked straight at the circle of light. I moved the circle like a line from the fishing pole down the wall and past his feet and out the window to the roof. He waited for it to stop moving and then started on his way to the window. I backed away from him. Halfway out the window he got stuck for a few seconds on his stomach. His fingers grasped at the light for something to pull himself up. He was having such a hard time that I thought about taking hold of his arms and helping him out to the rain. But I had the feeling that dragging his body through the window would have somehow humiliated him in front of the light that he was trying so hard to remember how to master. I waited for him to understand and hold still. When he had stopped reaching for the light and was starting to close his eyes I moved the light ever closer to him— just past the reach of his arms, which lunged forward for the last time to touch it. I knew he was free before he knew. He stood on the roof in the rain.

He was not still for long. He was on all fours again and crawling after the circle from the moment I started moving it flat across the surface of the roof. I moved the light an eternal step ahead of his grasping hands, so fast that he never caught it, so slow that he never lost hope that he was about to, drawing lines and stars and trees from one side of the roof to the other. He paused at last when I held the light motionless for a time in the corner of the roof. I heard him whining again. Lowering his face, so that his chin touched the floor, he watched the circle holding still in the rain, disappointed perhaps that it had given up running away from him and was waiting for him to make the last move. It might have been a trap. His finger touched the light for less than an instant before he sat up and shook his arm as if burned. I slid the light in a diagonal line away from him and far out into the water. He leaned forward on his hands and walked in silence to the edge without taking his eyes off the light.

His back was to me now. I walked right behind him and held the flashlight high like a torch, pointing the light downward at the water so that all he would have to do was fall into it. His fingers held tight to the edge of the roof.

In the darkness he leaned his head out over the water and stared at the circle of light floating a fall away from him in the flat waves. "Go on," I said. He turned and looked up at me without understanding.

"That's your home," I said. "See?"

I pointed to the water and he turned back and resumed gazing at the light. A still moment passed in the raining wind. And then without moving he began again to make a long and mournful sound that went on and on growing louder and softer and higher and lower, speeding up and slowing down. How long this sound lasted and what it meant I wasn't sure. I felt at first as if he were asking me a question I no longer knew how to answer, but then I began to think—I was thinking in words—that perhaps what he really wanted was for me to make the same wordless, ceaseless chanting sound he was making. That he wanted me to join him.

"No," I said. "I'm not coming with you."

He didn't move. He didn't seem to believe me. I was beginning to feel sick of holding the light up at the same place. I had one free arm and and it occurred to me with a shock that all I had to do was push him into the water and that would be the end of it. I was already starting to raise my hand up. Leaning forward, I crouched a little and set my palm down gently on the back of his head. His head was soaked and scarred up. Inside it was nothing except an empty dark space, I sensed that. Touching him I sensed again how light he was—so much lighter than he looked from outside—and how little I needed to do to get rid of him forever. A flick of the wrist and he would fall over.

But I couldn't do it. I couldn't push him. I stood there for a long time holding my palm to the back of his head and listening to the sound and at a certain point the entire desire to push him disappeared and I began to feel instead that I was blessing him. I was telling him that he was free to leave or not to. Leaving or remaining—it all amounted somehow to the same endless action. He could do whatever he wanted. If he wanted to leave now he could always decide to come back another time. Nothing was ever going to change and everything was still the same as in the beginning.

I was certain of all this for a full instant. I was even certain that in his own string of words he was thinking the same long and circular thought as I was—singing it. In a single unbroken motion I took my palm back from his head and lowered the flashlight and stepped back. At that moment the sound ceased and his entire body seemed to harden and go still as something dead. As if it had been my hand that was holding him up all along he began to collapse forward and headfirst into the water.

I heard the water splash up after him. Then I walked along the edge of the roof and pointed the flashlight down at the surface for a few minutes to see if he was going to come back up.

After a while I decided he was gone for good and I sat on the edge of the roof thinking about what to do next. I wasn't going back inside. To pass the time I started a game of shining the flashlight directly into my eyes until I couldn't see anything, and then counting out how long it took until I recovered sight, but the blind feeling never lasted longer than a few seconds, and the batteries were starting to die. By now the rain had stopped and the light of dawn was becoming visible. I watched for the sun. Inside I heard Mother waking back up and singing a psalm about being poured out like water in the dust as she dressed for the day in the bedroom. She must have seen as soon as she looked out the window that I was sitting on the roof with my back to her. She never called my name, though, or asked if I was all right. At one point she leaned through the window and set a folded blanket— the same blanket she had given to the Savior last night— and a cup of hot water on the roof. "You're soaked," she said. "You're going to get sick again." I caped the blanket around me and sat with the cup burning between my two hands until she came outside with the fishing pole and the bucket. She already seemed to know everything.

"I had to," I said.

I think she might have nodded. She set the bucket down on the roof and stood with her back to me baiting the hook and looking out at the horizon. Then she swung the fishing pole behind her and ran the line far out into the waves for the fish to think it was something else. A fake worm was at the end. I watched the line trail a slow wake through the waves.

"He didn't belong to us," I said.

"Go get the graphs."

"Are you listening to me?"

"Yes," she said.

"He's gone. I let him go."

"I know," she said. "So we're starting over."

I sat on the windowsill staring at the back of her head. She was in that head. She was standing ten steps away from me at the edge of the roof and all at once I decided— a decision was made in me—to stand up and run hard at her and push her back into the water before she could turn around and see me. I would explain nothing. I would have the higher ground. And when she surfaced in the waves and tried to climb back up to the roof I would push her back down again without a word. I would keep pushing her head underwater every time she tried to come up and after a while—I saw all this happening, I saw it so completely that I sometimes think it *did* happen—she would give up and swim out of my reach. She wouldn't swim too far. She would circle around the house weeping and screaming and demanding to know what in the name of God I was doing this for. A thousand times she would ask for an explanation and I would never answer her. I was absolutely certain about that. I was certain that silence would hurt her more than words and that if I kept saying nothing she would eventually stop asking. And at that point she would start plotting. She would hope that if she stayed afloat long enough I might fall asleep and give her a chance to climb back up, but I wouldn't. I'd stand guard on the roof until I saw her go under and was sure that she was drowned. And I knew somehow that in one of the long moments before she lost consciousness she would begin to understand me. She would forgive me and even thank me. She would see in that moment that I was doing all this for her own good, even though in truth I wasn't. In truth I was just doing it because nothing was stopping me.

I was about to. I had the potential in me. I had stood up and was taking the first step toward her and would have taken another. But at that instant something took the worm at the end of her line—and I stopped without thinking to see what it was she was going to pull out. Her fishing pole bent down from her at the water and she crouched and reeled. I thought for a second that she had caught the

Savior again, but when she fought the line out I saw that it was just another fluke. She turned and lowered the line down in front of me. Without thinking I moved closer and pressed the sliding fluke down under my foot on the roof. Then I did the job she had taught me to do of holding it still and taking the hook out and making it understand. When I was finished I slid the fluke into the bucket and watched it lying flat and unmoving at the bottom. It had nowhere to move. Its eyes were out of line. There was not enough space between them. Mother pointed her finger through the surface of the water to touch its face where the hook had gone through. She knew about fish. She had been a fisher even before the flood and she told me one day that fluke are born with an eye on each side of the head like the others. She said as they grow older one eye moves to the other side and the skull twists after it. Then the fluke stops swimming upright. It settles to the bottom and catches what comes past. The upper side, she said, can change to all different colors, but the lower side—the side that faces the seafloor—ends up white and stays that way to death.

I was calmer now. I sat at the end of the roof. Imagining what I might do to her seemed to have rid me of the desire to do anything except sit there and look into space. She set the fishing pole down and sat next to me, leaning forward, with her elbows on her knees and her feet hanging at the water, and after a time she asked me to tell her what had happened. I said what I remembered. I had let him go because he wanted to leave.

"You didn't *let him go*," she said. "You cast him out."

I didn't say anything. I just stared at the water and waited for her to go on. Her hand touched the back of my head in the same way I had touched the Savior and when I moved out from under her she leaned back on the roof to lie down looking up at the clouds. Another sun was coming up. After a long silence she sat up again and looked straight at me and asked if perhaps I was disappointed in him for not being what I imagined he was going to be—if that was the real reason I had chased him out. I thought about it. "No," I said, although I wasn't sure what the difference was. I might just as easily have said yes.

She sat with her hand in her chin. As if she were talking to someone else she told me that the trick is God *wants* us to feel disappointed in this world. He wants us to think we belong somewhere better.

She looked at me and asked, "Do you understand?"

"No," I said. "I don't know."

"Think about it."

"I don't want to think about it."

"But I'm asking you to," she said.

I tried to think about it. I thought I understood her point. But I resisted the point behind it.

"It's the same thing," I said. "I don't see a difference."

"Right," she said. "No difference between what?"

"What God wants," I said. "What kind of world we think we're owed. This world and that world—I don't see how it matters unless there's a line between them. A place where the one world splits from the other. And if there's no place you can point to then it doesn't make a difference where we think we're supposed to be. It's just a lot of different words."

I was silent with her for a time. I waited for her to ask me another question. Instead she started humming a song I recognized as one of her psalms. "I'm leaving," I said, but I wasn't. I sat listening to her and watching the horizon. In my mind I pictured the Savior lying still as the fluke on the seafloor and staring up at the sunlit surface. If he wanted to come back she would be here and I would be there and that would be the end of the story.

I remembered her telling me long ago her theory about how William Miller died. According to her theory what had eaten William Miller in the forest was no Savior. It was just another wild animal. She believed moreover that Miller knew from the beginning that the animal stalking after him from the start was not the Savior and that the peace he accomplished in the permanent moment before he was devoured had nonetheless prevented him from fighting back or running from painful death. Miller saw in that moment, she said, that the famished animal needed his flesh more than he did. He had offered his body to it in the spirit of Christ on the cross and Abraham lowering the knife down on Isaac's screaming throat. It occurred to me then that remaining in our home despite the rising water was her way of claiming for both of us that passive spirit of willed and blinded and infinitely defiant obedience. Moving would have amounted in her mind to an admission that the flood was something other than a test—that we were less like Abraham trusting the invisible word of God than we were like Isaac bound to an actual rock and thrashing to get free from his maniacal father. And in my head I understood that. I understood it. I understood that the world was ending for everyone always and eventually we had to worship our ignorance of whatever was about to happen. But I felt nothing like Abraham must have felt on the mountaintop. I felt more like the poor ram that had replaced Isaac on the altar when God intervened. And when I thought of Christ on the cross, sacrificed, it seemed to depend somehow on the presence of the two criminals crucified to his right and left: the one who was saved, the one who was not saved. It seemed unfair to have forsaken the other, to have promised paradise at such an earthly price as repentance. Something permanent inside me admired the doubter, the one who wanted Christ to just fly away, even if that was not the way, just surprise us. Surprise God.

I stood up and she stopped humming.

"I mean it this time," I said. "I'm leaving."

"I know. Go ahead."

"I'm not coming back."

"I know," she said. "But you're not going to get anywhere either."

I stood at the edge of the roof, staring down at the dark blue water rocking up against the house. At that moment I wasn't imagining I might go far enough to reach higher land. If land was even out there I would go to it, but it wasn't what I wanted. I wanted just to show her. To swim long enough out that I lost all sight of our home—and she lost her sight of me—and then to go on swimming without looking back or listening to her cries until I was too tired to remember where I was from. In my mind I saw what would happen from above. I saw her real surprise when I leapt. I saw her thinking I would turn around any second and come back to the house. I saw her screaming for me to come back as I grew farther and farther away from her, farther and farther into the sea until I disappeared under the horizon.

"Go ahead," she said. "Jump in."

"I'm going to. Just give me a second."

"Don't think about it so much."

"I'm not thinking."

I dipped one foot down into the water and brought it back up. And I did the same with the other foot.

"Do you remember how to swim?"

"I think," I said. "Just keep moving, right?"

"You used to swim like a fish."

"I don't remember that."

"Me neither," she said.

"Maybe you're thinking of someone else."

"No," she said. "There isn't anyone else."

She looked up at me with a kind of sad concern. It was the same look she had given the Savior after she pulled the hook from his mouth.

And then she turned and resumed watching the horizon. She sat there for so long and in such total stillness that for a time I seemed to forget she was waiting for me.

At last she asked: "Are you leaving?"

"Yes," I said. "I'm leaving."

But I didn't move. I did not see myself move. I sat back down next to her on the roof, which was wet from the rain, and I held my hands over my face, and I stared through my fingers at the horizon ahead, watching the sun circle up from half under the water, from behind the water, and I waited for something in me to move. I waited. I thought perhaps if I stared long enough at the horizon I might catch the sun in the act of lifting higher, but it was like trying to watch a tree grow taller, and I kept on having to start over again from wherever I still was. I was still here. I could not believe that I had ever been elsewhere or that I had even moved from one place to another since the beginning. It was all one place and the place was still inside me, still, spinning still as the surface of a planet circling around a single point rising out and out from the center of the universe. Not that I knew the truth. Just imagining that I *could* know it was strange enough. That I could imagine planets and seas and Saviors and the faces of others like us—that I could see them moving outside me with*out* closing my eyes—that I could see here and there at the same time—was impossible.

Imagine that in the time before the flood, or perhaps after it, a forest stood here and a person exactly like me walked a worn path through the trees. He was searching for me. In his mind he was repeating a secret message. A sequence of sounds that someone absolutely else had told him to deliver to me a long time ago. But he had walked for so long now that he no longer remembered who had given him the message or the meaning of the sounds he was appointed to pronounce or the place where he was supposed to find me. He would go on searching for that place. He would search forever and he would never find out I was here in the house. I was watching him from the outside. I was all around him all the time.

Art in Heaven

I was searching for the cat. I sat alone in the woods behind Father's house drinking warm water from a plastic bottle. Identical moths landed on my arm a few inches
apart from one another and worked at the skin. I pinched
one by the wing and held it in front of me. Its free wing
flapped. For centuries philosophers have claimed that every living thing has an astral body that contains our real
mind. I uncapped the water bottle and let the moth go
inside. Enough water was at the bottom that when I replaced the cap and shook the bottle the moth was brought
down from the wall and drowned in the water. I pocketed
the bottle and followed the flags down the path that led
to Father's house. At the end of the path I passed the remains of a dead elm tree growing moss and flowers from
the trunk. In front of the trunk was a sign that described
the death of a tree as a gradual and magnificent transfor-

mation. Alone among living things they retain their character and dignity after death.

I walked out of the woods and into the house. In the living room Father reclined in a wooden rocking chair watching the six o'clock news. He might have said hello. I set the water bottle with the moth on the coffee table and sat on the sofa waiting for him to judge me. Inside the television a newsman reported that a twelve-hundred pound buffalo had escaped from a farm in the late hours of last night. No one knew where the buffalo was. But someone claimed to have seen him at the intersection between First Street and Second. He had sprinted away from the headlights of an approaching car.

"So you're still an atheist," said Father.

"I think so."

"But you believe in life."

"I have experiential evidence of life."

"But God is life," he said.

"Okay. Then I believe in God."

We watched the television. A photograph of the buffalo grazing in a yellow sunlit field appeared on the screen. He had no opinions either way about God. He could outrun the fastest living human and leap over a six foot tall barbed-wire fence despite his size. Father rocked forward in his rocking chair and picked up the water bottle from the coffee table. I watched him uncap the bottle and bring an eyeball to the open lid. Not letting go of the bottle he leaned back in his chair looking at the television.

"You are not your brain," he declared.

"I know," I said. "I never said I was."

"And you're not a god either."

"I know," I said. "I'm a person."

"And you agree that a person is more than a plant?"

"I think so. I don't know what that means—*more than*."

"I mean you're created in the image of God. You can *think*." He looked away from the television for the first time since I had come into the room—right at me. I remembered a magazine article about a renowned botanist who claimed that certain plants felt pain. But before I could mention this article Father had stood from his rocking chair and walked to the wilted peace lily on the windowsill. "This peace lily," he said, "cannot think about the afterlife. It cannot formulate mathematical equations. It cannot will itself to move a leaf. You see that, don't you?" He lifted a yellow-edged leaf with the hand that held the bottle. Examining the leaf he motioned for me to move the rocking chair to the windowsill and sit. He let go of the leaf and the stem fell without a fight. "Now I want you to do something for me," said Father after I sat down. "I want you to remain in this chair for the next hour. No looking out the window. No closing your eyes. For the next hour I want you to focus on nothing except this peace lily." He poured the water with the remains of the moth into the pot. Then he poured more water into the pot from a pitcher on the windowsill. "Consider what deliberate results are produced by this unconscious plant."

He walked behind me and turned the television off in the middle of a warning about what to do if we saw the buffalo. I never got to hear how many Americans had been killed by bison in the last year alone.

In the new silence I rocked back and forth in the chair watching the peace lily take the water in.

"Do I really have to do this?" I asked.

"Not unless you're a determinist."

"I already know what happens."

"Are you sure about that?"

"It comes back to life," I said. "The leaves stand up again."

He forced a laugh out. He had a policy of not responding to me if I sounded too certain. He rose from the sofa and went out the back door to the lawn. Through the window behind the peace lily I saw him scoop dry cat food from a paper grocery bag into the dish for the missing cat. He called for the cat a few times. Then he knelt in the grass facing the forest and began to pray with his palms on his knees and his back to the window.

Watching him pray was more interesting than watching the Peace Lily revive. I wondered where his spirit was. I remembered him telling me once that during prayer he sometimes attained such a state of concentration that he was able to depart from his flesh and view his body from above. He compared the sight of his body praying to that of an autumn leaf floating on the surface of a pond.

I watched for his spirit to rise. After the hour was passed I noticed the leaves of the peace lily were starting to lift. But I had not caught a single leaf in the act of movement. I was too fast for a plant. I went out the back door and walked to the place where Father prayed. His eyes were open at the woods. When he saw me he went back to his body and signed the cross. I sat in the grass beside him and watched the trees.

"Did you see it move?"

"I think so," I said.

"How did it move?"

"The leaves lifted up."

"But who lifted the leaves?"

"The peace lily," I said.

"But the peace lily is unconscious. How can an unconscious plant perform such a comprehensive action?" He asked as though he really wanted a conclusive answer. But I knew that whatever I answered would provoke another question. Even if I admitted God had moved the peace lily he would ask me to explain what the word *God* meant. And if I argued that the resurrection of the peace lily was nothing more than a reaction to the roots taking the water in he would force me to trace that reaction back to an omnipotent and omniscient First Cause—an unmoved mover. I knew what he wanted me to say. The power that allows a plant to move will not abandon humanity to its own devices.

"I'm just saying I don't know," I said. "That's all I'm saying."

I picked at the grass in front of me. Father remained silent listening to the wind swell around the trees. His eyes were wide and unblinking and anchored on an expanse of grass where absolutely nothing was going on. Now and then he nodded and once he shook his head and lifted an index finger as if to correct an argument he had never really listened to. "I read something the other night about Socrates," he said. "I read that he used to stand in the streets of Athens just thinking. I mean just totally lost in thought. For *hours*." He looked at me. "You ever try to do that? Just think?"

"No."

"Try it."

"Try to think?"

"Try to *keep* thinking. That's the hard part."

I looked at the line of evergreens that separated the

backyard from the forest. Something about the trees reminded me of a bedtime story Father had told me when I
was a child in which a lone astronaut named Noah piloted
a small rocket away from the mothership and toward an
empty planet in another solar system. In his spacecraft
Noah had brought thousands of sealed boxes containing
the seeds of every plant rescued from the dying earth,
which had been abandoned just before the sun was sched-
uled to supernova. His task when he reached the new and
barren planet, which Father called Tortoise, was to plant
and nourish the seeds so that the human and animal pas-
sengers on the mothership following a few years behind
him would have a head start in founding a new civiliza-
tion when they landed. But for some reason I have since
forgotten—some catastrophic miscalculation or malfunc-
tion—the mothership self-destructed in space a few hours
after Noah descended. He sat in the control room of his
rocket watching the screen showing the inside of the ship
explode into a pure white light that blacked out into static.
A few seconds of screaming played on the radio before
cutting off forever.

"See," said Father. "You can't."

"I can. I'm thinking."

"About what?"

"Time," I said.

"Time is an illusion," he said.

"I was thinking how old I'm getting."

"You're twenty-three."

"I was wondering what I'll be doing when I'm thirty-
three."

I watched the evening darken the grass. In the story
Noah was pushing open the door of his rocket and survey-

ing through binoculars the cratered landscape of Tortoise. A minute's walk away from him the waves of the Tortoisian Ocean crested like all other waves onto a shore devoid of seashells. Nothing had ever lived in that ocean— he knew that. A mathematical formula written many generations before the exodus from earth had already established that the chances of even single-celled organisms arising elsewhere in the universe were nil. Yet the atmosphere of Tortoise was so elementally similar to that of earth that Noah could reasonably hope at least some of the seeds would take root and spread earth-life across the land. Walking to the shore of the ocean he wondered if his original mission of planting the seeds was worth completing. He already knew the ending. Even the unborn stars at the outer rims of the universe were eventually going to burn themselves out.

"In ten years," said Father, "you're going to save the world."

"Okay."

"I'm serious."

"I know. I believe you."

In a way I did. I had no reason not to. If God was life then even the last human in the universe was divine. Noah, I remembered, had come to a similar conclusion as he stared at the receding waves of Tortoise. He had walked back from the shore to his rocket parked among the rocks and retrieved from the refrigerated Seed Room a metal box marked EVERGREENS. In the damp soil behind the shoreline he shoveled a hole and buried a single pine seed from the box. He planted no more seeds that day. He returned to his rocket. Fearing that he might finish his work too soon and have nothing left to live for

Noah had resolved to make a ritual of planting just a single new seed at the same time each morning. He stuck to this ritual for thousands of years. During that time he watched the seeds grow into a self-perpetuating forest so vast and intricate that he couldn't find his way out of it. In the daylight hours he would walk paths through the trees calling out for help and hoping—though he knew there was no hope—that he might hear another person calling back to him or see a tree creature staring down at him from the branches or a hawk gliding above the clouds. But nothing seemed to see or hear him and after many years of searching he began to suspect that the people and animals he remembered from earth were nothing more than inventions of his imagination and that he had in fact lived on Tortoise from the beginning and would remain there to the end. His sole defense against this constant suspicion was to remember the bagful of maple seeds that he had brought from earth—the last of the original stock— and that he still carried with him wherever he went. At night he held these seeds in sleep.

"You must *want* to," said Father. "You must think about it."

"Never," I said. "Not once."

"You're lying. You're afraid to admit it."

"Why would I think about saving the world?"

"Because," he said, "here we are. Shit, when I was your age I thought about nothing else." He reached in his coat and pulled out a pipe and a plastic bag of tobacco that he loaded into the end. "I had a theory about Jesus," he said, lighting the pipe. "That he was acting. That he was just an ordinary guy and he knew it. All along he knew it. No virgin mother. No wise men following a star to a manger in Bethlehem. Bullshit. I figured Jesus was just some dreamy kid who'd read the prophets. Saw what the world was waiting for. The world was waiting for a messiah so he said okay. Sure. I can do that. If no one else wants to, sure, I will. Watch me. Everyone watch me. I'm the messiah!"

"But he wasn't."

"He *was*. He absolutely was. That was the trick. Jesus was the only one who got it. God wasn't going to *send* his son. God was waiting just like everyone else. Waiting for someone to call him father. Whoever called him father was his son. Whoever played the part won the part. That simple." He laughed one syllable. "So I thought about it. I thought, okay: Jesus won the part. Jesus beat me to it. Fine. But now here we are again. Here we've been for two thousand years. Same situation as before except this time we know what we're waiting for. We're waiting for the Second Coming. And we figure when he gets here he'll say who he is and save what he saves and that will be that. Should I shut up?"

"No," I said. "I'm interested."

"You think I'm lying?"

"No," I said. "You never lie."

"Good," he said. "Wait. What was I saying?"

"He'll come again in glory to judge the living and the dead."

"Right," he said. "Right, but he won't. He won't come again to judge anything. Not Jesus, anyway. Jesus already did his job. Someone else is up."

"You're up."

"I thought I was," he said. "I really did. Only I had no idea what the hell I was supposed to do. I had to tell everyone I was God's son, but how? How do you get a person to believe that? How do you get *God* to believe that? I took another look at the Gospels—at what Jesus had done. Jesus had pretty much just one day up and decided to start preaching. Before that he was anonymous as I am. He was nobody. And of course nobody would have trusted a word he said if not for the fact he backed it up. He performed miracles. That was the proof. And that was the precedent I had to follow. If I could cure the sick or walk on water then people would pay attention to me. *God* would pay attention to me. Otherwise what am I? I'm a fraud. I'm phonier than Satan."

He set the pipe on the wooden floor of the porch. As the smoke rose from the bowl of the pipe and vanished into the past he reached a hand into his coat pocket and scrounged out the wallet I had bought him for a birthday gift a few years back. I watched him linger through the eight photos I had arranged chronologically in the wallet album—each one flattering him at different ages running from oldest to youngest. After a while he picked out a snapshot from thirty years ago of him at a Halloween party wearing a white robe and a pair of wings crafted from the flaps of a cardboard box and painted cloud white. He was pretending not to pose for the camera. In the center of a cornfield he stood gazing at the setting sun as if sizing up an enemy.

"This was right after I got out of college," he said, showing me the photo. "I'm still living at home. I'm confident—I know I'm right, I know what I want to do for the world—but I'm a lot like you are now: Quiet. I'm not about to come out and declare that I'm the messiah. Not yet anyway. First I have to prepare. I have to get away for a while and figure out what kind of Christ I want to become. It's part of the test. In the Gospels Jesus goes off to the desert and fasts for forty days and forty nights. He passes the test. He tells Satan to go home. And after that he knows what he is.

"So one night I write a runaway note to my parents. Dear Mom and Dad: Don't look for me. That's pretty much all I tell them. And I walk out of the house with nothing but a bag of clothes and a notebook. At this point I'm still planning to head west—to the first desert I can find. I'm hitchhiking. But as soon as the second car passes without pulling over I put my thumb down. I change my mind. I figure the desert part isn't important. Place isn't important. What's important is that I find someplace isolated—someplace no one will come and interrupt me. That's all God cares about. So instead of the desert I decide to just head over to the beach.

"Back then the beach is different. The houses are spread out. In the woods above the dunes was a cave I had discovered as a kid. I was always afraid to go into the cave because I couldn't see the back of it. I didn't know how deep it was. This time, though, I go right in and it turns out that wall's just about ten feet back. Perfect. I sit down against the wall and look out at what I can see of the water. Hours pass. I don't move. I don't sleep. And I don't do any praying either. I don't even think about anything in particular. I'm thinking of this whole process as more a matter of physical endurance than anything spiritual. I figure if I just stay where I am in the cave without eating or drinking or talking to anyone else then eventually my body will start to break down. I'll start to die. And when that happens—when I'm right between life and death—

the devil's going to show up and offer me whatever I want. All I have to do then is decline. I just have to look him in the head and say: No."

He put the wallet back in his pocket and pulled another line of smoke from the pipe. A robin landed on the bird-feeder nailed to the trunk of the maple and picked at the seeds. He stood and took a few careful steps toward the tree. Among his listed plans for the summer was to catch a bird in his bare hands and release it inside the house. But the robin flew away before he even had a chance to reach for it. He leaned back against the trunk of the maple looking up into the branches.

"After a while," he went on, "I'm starting to think about heading home. I'm hungry. I want to sleep. Worst of all I'm worrying about my father. I know he's searching for me. I have this premonition—this repeating image—of him posting a picture of me on the telephone pole across the street from our house. What depresses me about this image is the word written in big letters above the picture: MISSING. It's a statement of fact: Nobody knows where I am. I understand that. But as time passes I start to read the word as an accusation. I start to see the poster as an advertisement of what I'm feeling. I miss him. I miss home. I do. Giving up seems more and more like the moral decision. God *wants* me to give up. He wants me to get up and to walk back to my house and apologize for what a self-centered little clown I've become. I'm convinced. I'm moving."

I waited for him to go on. He stood smoking under the maple a few feet from the porch and staring at the space above me—perhaps at his own smoking reflection staring back at him from the sliding glass door.

"You seen the cat?" he asked.

"No."

"She abandoned us."

"That's because you put her in that cage."

I looked at the woods. I meant for him to remember the night when the cat was hunting a moth orbiting the light bulb that hung from the kitchen ceiling. Pouncing from the ledge on top of the cabinets, she had somehow swiped the light out of its socket and broke the bulb all over the floor. As I lit candles and swept the shards into the dustpan Father had jailed the cat inside the cardboard box we had once brought the television home in. He set the box on the living room carpet and kept her imprisoned for the next three days, policing the room the entire time and camping out on the sofa at night to keep me from letting her go. From bed the first night I heard the cat crying and scratching lines in the walls. At a certain point, though, she gave up, and when Father at last permitted me to open the box, I saw her curled sleeping at the bottom—blinking awake at the light. She stayed in the box for another few seconds before she leapt out to look for something else.

"It's not a cage," he said. "It's an extension."

I listened to him call for her to come back from the forest. Nothing moved the wind. A low moon held full above the pines. One night on the lawn a long time ago Father had pointed at a younger version of that same moon and said that if I looked close I could see the American flag the astronauts from the first Apollo landing had planted on the surface. I believed him at the time. I still swear I saw the flag billowing red and white in the lunar wind. But a few nights later in the same place on the lawn he

said there was no flag on the moon—that the moon landing had in fact been staged in a secret film studio. He said
that the moon and stars were illusions and that what we
saw in the nighttime sky was really nothing more than
a *subjective projection of our three dimensional imaginings*.
No one had really *landed* on the moon. No one had even
moved a centimeter since the beginning of time. Humans
were as capable of moving from one place to another as a
written word was of leaping off a page.

"So you gave up," I said.

"I missed home."

"You left the cave."

"No," he said. "I was *about* to leave the cave." He walked
back to the porch and reclaimed his place beside me. "But
as soon as I stand up to leave I stop and start thinking
again. I think about it for a while and I figure out I've been
fooled. I've fooled myself. That voice tempting me to go
back home—that was the voice of the *devil*: disguised as
discretion. I remember the scene in Matthew when Satan
takes Jesus to the top of a mountain and offers him all
the Kingdoms of the world. Away with you, Jesus says.
And that's what I say now. *No*. I keep saying it: *No*. After
a while the word becomes a wall that stops me from remembering anything. Not just my parents and the poster
and the fact that I'm missed: I forget God. I forget that
I'm even flesh. I'm not. I'm nothing but a voice in the
wilderness affirming the good news: *no, no, no*."

He mouthed the word *no* a few more times without letting the sound out. Then he studied the smoke rising up
from his pipe into the night as if noticing for the first time
that smoke seems to disappear—just disappear. I thought
at first he was going to go on. But his method had always

been to end before the ending. In the Tortoise story Noah had ended up deciding to stop searching for others. He had gone out to the most fertile soil in the forest and dug a hole that was just deep and wide enough for him to lie down in without feeling stuck. He had lain flat on his back at the bottom of the hole and held the maple seeds from earth in his fists and looked up at the sky. The first stars were coming out. Through the night he stared at the stars and thought nothing except that he was here. He was never going to move again. His plan was to stare and stare until he grew still and silent as the maple seeds in his hands—to grow into and out of the seeds and become part of the growing trees.

"That's the end?" I asked.

"That's the *midpoint*."

"Then what happens?"

"The midpoint explodes."

"I mean what happens to you?"

"Nothing," he said. "I grow bigger and bigger."

"So you gave up then. You went back home."

"No," he said. "I'm still in that cave right now."

I asked him no more questions. I already knew his answers. Next to his bed he kept a marbled notebook that he waked for in the morning or night to pencil-sketch the last images he remembered from his receding dreams. Coming into his room to give him a handshake goodnight, I sometimes found him leaned beneath the covers examining his most recent drawing. I was never allowed to look at the pictures; he hid them from me. Sometimes when I opened the door he would cross an index finger over his lips and open his palm to hold me still. From the door I watched him tilt the page as if searching for an angle that might somehow enable him to glimpse the picture from the back or the side—in three dimensions. His expression when he considered his art was neither proud nor disappointed. No judgment was passed. More than anything he appeared perplexed and perhaps ashamed that his sleeping mind had birthed such images without consulting the rest of him. I recognized this expression of shame and perplexity and absolute incomprehension when he looked at me now. He reached an arm and touched the back of my head.

"I *invented* you," he said.

"I know."

"You don't understand," he said.

"I do," I said. "You're God."

I waited for him to get his hand off me, watching the pines that walled the forest—were the forest. From the space between two of the pines, the runaway buffalo appeared, his eyes lowered at the earth. His head reminded me of the molded trunk of the dead elm. I watched him graze at the moonlit grass no more than a long tree's length away from us. He looked like every other buffalo I had ever seen. I could have imagined him. And yet if we all joined together to make a living animal out of nothing we would eventually give up. I turned to Father. His eyes were closed. "If we move," he said, "he might run away." We sat stiller than plants inside our separate bodies.

Action at a Distance

I was older than I was in the beginning. I was practic-
ing remaining in the moment after the end. Marie had
gone outside to the garden and I passed her on the way
to the path through the woods to the water. She stood at
the apple tree holding a big glass jar filled with beetles
pinched out from the leaves. The cat was curled awake
on top of the picnic table on the porch and I motioned for
him to come with me instead of her. He fell behind at first
to climb up a tree and then climbed down and curved past
me around the run of the path to the beach. I met him
again when I got to the beach. No one else was there. A
rowboat rocked in the waves without getting out from the
anchor. I sat at the high tide line and breathed in. Breathing out I began repeating the name of God. I had read
somewhere that if I sat still and said the name of God over
and over again I would escape from time. But I couldn't
get past a few repetitions before the mosquitoes got to

me and I started thinking Marie had followed me down the path and was watching me from the trees and taking notes. I dug a stone from the sand and turned around. In the reeds the cat was pouncing after sand bugs. He ran back to hunt for the sound of the stone I pitched deep into the pine trees. I followed him over the dunes and back down the path to the house. Back in the garden Marie was sitting at the picnic table on the porch and writing a love letter to me in her notebook. A glass jar on the table was filled with the beetles she had taken from the leaves. I sat across from her and asked what she was writing about me and she said just words.

"Can I read them?"

"No."

"Read it to me then."

"No," she said. "I'm not finished."

She covered the page with her palm. I walked back into the garden to pick something from a tree.

Nested on the underside of the leaf I picked was a cluster of orange beetle eggs she must have missed when she went around with the jar. If I stared at the eggs long enough a pack of humpbacked larvae would hatch and grow holes through the leaves. I picked a pockmarked apple and sat in the shade watching her writing.

"Do you still believe in reincarnation?"

"I think so," she said.

"So you're a Buddhist."

"No. I don't know."

"Then why do you believe in it?"

She went back to writing.

I watched the line of trees that kept the garden from the forest. Behind the trees were trees and trees to the water. No others. No one lived around us. She had moved us here to hear the birds and see the stars better at night. How long since we moved I sometimes forgot.

"Do you remember your last life?"

"Sometimes," she said.

"Did you know me?"

"I knew everyone."

"I'm asking if you knew me."

"I don't know," she said.

"That doesn't make sense."

"Okay."

"I'm just saying."

"Okay. I'm trying to write."

I was competing with the page. Winning her attention was just a matter of making a scene.

I closed my eyes and posed as a man lost in meditation, mouthing the name of God as I had on the beach. I was thinking she might draw me. In bed one night, as we waited for sleep, she had listed *artist* among the paths she might go down in her next life: scientist, shepherd, shoemaker, magician. But when I broke in to remind her that she still had time to become another person in *this* life she had turned away from me to face the wall. After a while I heard her weeping. I tried to talk her back to me. I asked her to remember how old Adam was when he died in the book. All the days that Adam lived were nine hundred and thirty years. And then he died. We still had eight hundred and ninety seven to go if we lived that long. Beneath the apple tree remembering I multiplied twelve by thirty-three and added another three for April, May, and June: three hundred and ninety nine was the number of months we had lived.

I had to see how long that was. I pictured a flat number line floating in space and spaced from zero to four hundred and arrowed out from both ends to the ends of the known universe. Sixty seconds for each minute. But the lines between the seconds were black holes with spaces at the bottom.

I lifted my eyes open before I fell in. Marie was leaning back in her chair and looking at me as though there was something there.

She asked what I was doing.

"Thinking," I said.

"No you're not."

"I am."

"Thinking about what?"

"Time," I said. "I was thinking how old we are."

No response. I watched her read back through what she had written. To prove I was telling the truth I tried to think of something old about her. I thought of a night I found her in the garden watching—

"The stars," I said.

"What?"

"You used to look at the stars."

"I still look at the stars."

"That's what I was remembering."

"It's not a memory if I still do it."

"I was remembering that one night you thought they were falling."

That was a start. She was stopping to listen to me. I moved to the table with her eyes on me and sat in the chair across from where she was. Still the notebook was open. Another word or two and then she closed the notebook with the pen at the page she was in the middle of.

Now I would have to go on. Start with the astronomy book and from there to the falling stars and sleepwalking: after that I would remember the ending back again. I picked up the jarful of beetles from the table and watched them sticking to the clear glass walls and climbing for the top. No one knew what glass was.

"You remember that night?"

"You're lying."

"I'm not."

"I don't know."

"It was a while back," I said. "I think it was the summer we moved here. You were reading that book about the universe that summer—that big astronomy book with all the new satellite pictures of planets and galaxies. And one of the things you read in the book was that back in the time before electricity and light pollution the night used to look totally different from earth. Back then, you said, the stars looked so bright that people thought the Milky Way was like some continuous spilled liquid. Like the galaxy was an oozing flood of light. And I remember you telling me this one night when we were sitting right here: that people didn't use to think of the stars as *separate* the way we do nowadays. That they used to think of space more like we think of the ocean now—like a single flowing substance. And from that point on you became more and more obsessed with *space*. You kept talking about what you were reading in the book. About how many stars there were and how long their light was. How enormous the universe was and how little we really knew about anything. You talked so much about the stars that after a while I started feeling jealous of them. I felt like you were becoming more interested in the universe than in me."

"I was."

"You still are. But at the time that scared me. I was scared you were starting to see how average I was. How uninterested. To me the stars were just stars. Nothing you said changed the way I saw them."

"I knew that."

"But I *wanted* to change. I acted interested because I wanted to care as much as you did. I wanted to feel what you felt. I thought if we had the same exact feelings we would eventually become the same person. That was what I wanted back then." I paused. "And so one night I wake up and you aren't in bed with me. You're gone. And the first thought I had was that you had left me and gone back to the real world. I was paranoid—I know. I searched the house before I went outside and found you in the garden. You were lying on your back under the apple tree with the book open on your chest. Not reading the book. Just squinting through the branches at the sky as if you were trying to make out something very small in the distance. You remember yet?"

"No."

"You wouldn't," I said. "I remember I turned the porch light on and walked over so you could see me. I asked you what you were looking at and after a second or two you turned your head toward me. Your head turned very slowly. So slowly that I had the feeling for a second it was connected to strings. I had this feeling someone was pulling you from outside like a puppet. You know what you said?"

"You're making this up."

"I'm not," I said.

"I would remember."

"You wouldn't," I said. "You wouldn't because you were *sleepwalking*. I figured that out soon as I saw you in the eyes. I saw from the second you turned to me that you weren't inside them. You weren't recognizing me as me. Yet you were still aware of what was going on. You were aware enough to answer the question I asked you. And what you told me when I looked at you—and I swear to God I'm not making this up—was that you were waiting for the end of time. That time was about to end. You said when time ended the stars were going to fall down on the earth and the Savior was going to burst through the night and come down in a fiery chariot and take us home. What are you laughing at?"

"Nothing," she said.

"This isn't a joke."

"I know."

"This is serious," I said. "I was seriously afraid of you. Not afraid that you were out of your mind. No, I was afraid because for the first second I *believed* you. And I remember for that first believing second I had this hollowed-out feeling inside. A feeling I couldn't breathe. I looked up expecting to see the stars falling down on us and landing like little hailstones on the grass. But nothing was there. And the stillness of the stars calmed me back down after a while. I sat down alongside you and leaned back in the grass. And I decided then not to take your hand or even talk for a while—to just lie in the grass watching the stars until we fell asleep.

"So to pass the time I took the book from the grass and opened to your bookmark. You had been reading the chapter about the Flat Earth Theory—the theory that the earth wasn't a sphere but a flat disc floating in empty space. Hell was about a hundred miles underneath the earth according to the flat-earthers and the stars and planets were just three thousand miles above us. Heaven was not a state of mind or a separate universe but an actual physical space that existed above the stars. If we built a spaceship and traveled high enough, the book said, we would actually arrive in Paradise."

I was stuck. The cat leapt onto her lap. His eyes closed when she scratched his chin.

I reached across the table and took the notebook open. *I've been thinking over.* I read another few words *what you said and* from lower down on the page *floating freely* before she stood reaching and snatched the notebook *about heaven* back out of my hands. I could have held on to it if I wanted to. But I really just wanted her to look at me as if she believed.

"You've been thinking over," I said.

"Stop," she said.

"Thinking what?"

"Just finish the story."

"You were thinking about heaven."

"No. Just finish—"

"Can I read it when I'm done?"

"No," she said. "I don't know. Just finish the story."

She was listening to herself. She once said that she loved me *as much as* she loved the rest of God. I was supposed to translate that as enough.

"Fine," I said, "the flat earth theory." I thought about it. "The strange part was that the flat earth theory was a pretty recent one. It started about two hundred years ago when this philosopher named Parallax—a pseudonym; I forget his real name—wrote a four-hundred-page book called *Earth Not a Globe*. His basic argument was that the Copernican model of the universe was totally speculative. That if we stopped speculating and investigated the world through experiment—if we just figured out how to set up the right *kinds* of experiments—we would see beyond doubt that the earth was in fact a flat disc. And he gave a lot of evidence for this argument. He drew a lot of diagrams that seemed to back his evidence up. And he anticipated all the questions the round-earthers—he called them *globularists*—were going to come at him with. His explanation of gravity was that the earth and stars were accelerating *upwards* like an elevator at an equal and constant rate. His answer to the question of how come no one falls over the edge of the earth was to simply point to his map of the flat earth: North Pole at the center and Antarctica all around the perimeter. Antarctica, he said, was a wall of ice that comprised the entire circumference of the earth. He said Magellan had just traveled a big circle around the surface of the disk like the fingers of a clock.

"And so anyway I'm reading this next to you on the lawn. So focused on what I'm reading I forget about you for a while. Parallax is all I think about for now. And even though I know how wrong he was, how the pictures of earth from outer space prove him wrong, a part of me wonders if he was on to something. I start having this *how-do-I-know* feeling. You know? I start asking myself how I know for sure that the earth is round in the first place. How I even know that earth *exists*. All I know for certain—and I know you know this too—all I know is that *I* exist. That's all. And I stop reading when I remember this. I feel calmed out when I remember this, as if for once I don't need to *go* anywhere. I close my eyes and fall asleep thinking about how absolutely I exist. How even if nothing else is real—even if everything I think is one big lie—I'm still the one being lied to and living that lie. Either that or I'm the liar. And this thought starts me dreaming. I start dreaming about a flood taking up the entire earth. But before I can fall all the way into the dream I hear this *sound*." I reached for the jar of beetles. "You remember the sound?"

"No."

"Try to."

"No," she said. "I can't."

I twisted open the jar and lowered an eye at the opening. Then I pinched a beetle out and set it down walking on the table.

"At first," I said, twisting the top back on the jar, "the sound is like something crashing in the woods. I wake up hearing this tremendous roar of crunching metal and glass breaking into thousands of pieces. And then when the crashing fades out another sound starts to replace it. It sounds like the voice of something deep in the woods screaming out for help. Screaming *words*—I'm certain of that. Except that I can't make out what the words mean or where the voice is coming from. I seem to hear it coming from every direction at the same time."

The beetle was almost at the edge of the table. I picked it back up and left it in the center to begin again.

"And so I'm listening to this sound. I'm sitting right there listening to it getting louder. And then I look at you in the grass and you're just lying on your back like before. Except now your eyes are wide open white and absolutely still. Not blinking. Not once blinking. In your face is this faraway expression of focused and complete disappointment. Not like you're waiting for a vision from the heavens but like the vision you were waiting for has come and gone too quickly for you to make sense of it. You're stiller than a plant. I say your name—nothing. Shake you—no response. I take your wrist. At first nothing, but then after a second I feel a pulse trip through. But your arm deadens back on the grass like a plank of wood when I let go. And you lie there in the grass like some dead thing staring at the sky. Like someone flicked an off switch in the back of your brain. I look up. In the sky I see the clouds gathered against one another and a bird gliding still against the clouds. A hawk: I can tell from the tail. I watch the hawk for less than an instant before I start to feel as if I'm looking at a picture of a hawk. Because it's not moving—the hawk. And neither are the branches or the clouds or the wind. Nothing moves anymore except me."

I looked at her with my entire face. She was paying more attention to the cat on her lap than to me.

"I'm not making this up," I said.

"I know."

"I swear to God I'm not."

"I know," she said. "I didn't say you were."

She was acting like I was. I was acting like I cared what she thought.

I said nothing for a long time and for no good reason. A feeling was hardening against her inside me.

She reached for her pen and took the notebook open to a blank page in the back. On the opened page she started drawing a picture of what I looked like from the outside. Nothing she ever did surprised me. Not even in the beginning. But one night she asked me to describe her in one word and the first one I thought of was *new*. Her word for me was *no*.

"You have a bad memory," I said.

"Okay."

"You really do," I said.

"Fine," she said. "Why does that matter?"

It mattered because our minds were made of a certain number of parts. As time passed we sometimes had to make repairs, discarding old parts and replacing them with new and sturdier ones. But if we kept replacing old parts with new parts we would eventually find that our original minds were gone. God would no longer remember us.

"Change is constant," I said.

She ignored me. She worked on her drawing for another while before she held the page up.

It was a picture of me meditating under the apple tree. In the picture I was thinking from a cartoon bubble pointed at my head. *I'm not making this up*, I was thinking. *I swear to God I'm not.*

"That's not me," I said.

She went back to petting the cat, staring past me and at the darkening trees.

She used to fantasize about both of us abandoning speech and becoming like deer in the woods. I would love her without having to think the word *love*. I would give endlessly without knowing that I was *giving*.

"It's not," I said.

A moment slowed past us. I turned the porch light on and walked another moment back to the garden to get away from her.

The porch looked like a stage fallen silent after the curtain parted. She was acting alone and thought-drowned, her chin rested on her open palm as her other arm cradled the cat. Her role was to remain Marie. Mine was to go back to the porch and tell her the rest of the story.

In the story I would have told her I was lying. I would have said the sound and everything after that was in fact a dream I was in without her. That time had gone still in the dream and I was stuck inside that stillness even now and searching for something outside me to move. I would have gone on and on. But as I started to speak I remembered I had already performed this exact scene at some remote time in the recorded past. I wasn't sure when or where. I only knew I was about to make the same mistake I had made last time.

"Did this happen before?"

"What?"

"This," I said. "I did this once before."

"I know," she said. "You didn't know that?"

She let the cat go out from her arms. He bounded off her lap and angled his face high at a moth hovered around the light. In his eyes were calculations about how to catch the moth if he could leap as high as the light. But there was nothing for him to leap from. The floor was on the floor.

"I feel dizzy," I said.

"Sit down."

"I can't."

"Take a deep breath."

"I can't do this anymore."

"You're not doing anything."

"I am," I said. "I keep thinking the same thoughts."

I was about to fall down. I walked back to the porch and picked up the jar of beetles for something to hold on to.

Inside the earth was spinning the moon out above the trees. A certain star was four light years away from us. Past the stars were the walls of the universe speeding out from the center at the speed of light. Into what I would never picture. Once as we looked at the sky she had asked if I thought there were other worlds out there. I thought there were an infinite number.

"It's the same thing over and over again," I said.

"Then do something new," she said. "Surprise me."

In my hand the jar of beetles was starting to feel like something to throw. If I threw the jar at her I could remind her that she had dared me to do something new. Not that I wanted to hurt her. I just wanted to prove somehow that I was a god. I held the jar up so that the light from the light went through and out the other side. I had to imagine the universe as something like the *surface* of a gigantic balloon growing bigger and heavier and longer. No matter how many times I circled the surface I would never reach an edge to leap from. I wound back and pitched the jar hard and fast at the floor.

There.

She stared at the shards. I should not have. But the breaking sound had paid for more than whatever remorse I felt now. I felt more like I was breathing in for the first time after screaming out from the bottom of a black sea.

Her face was a wall. Her feet walked bare around the broken glass to the screen door inside the house.

"Your leg's bleeding," I said.

The door slung hard behind her. Some of the beetles had gone still to death amidst the glass. I watched the survivors radiate out from the midpoint, each one lining a crooked path across the porch and toward the garden.

Their minds were too small to thank me for letting them go.

Marie shouldered through the door holding the broom and dustpan and another jar.

"*Move*," she said.

I leaned against the door watching her sweep. She swept around the living beetles to gather the dead ones together in the pile of glass.

"Go away," she said.

"I'm sorry."

"No you're not."

"I feel better now."

"Good," she said.

"Are you mad at me?"

"No."

"I still want to read your letter."

"Good."

"Can I read it?"

"Go away," she said. "Go lie down."

I went inside to the living room. In the dark I flattened down on the floor and looked up at the ceiling.

I didn't know what to do. After a while I closed my eyes and tried to sleep. I was thinking for some reason about something Parallax had said about the surface of the earth. If earth was a globe then every part of the surface must curve downward like the arc of a circle. Every part must become part of the arc. If earth's circumference was twenty-five-thousand miles then the surface would curve farther and farther down from whatever point of the arc I was on. I was doing the math. If the math was right the earth would arc down eight inches for the first mile and thirty two inches for the second and seventy two inches for the third, fourth, fifth. After a few miles the curvature would become so obvious I would have no problem detecting it.

I heard the door open. I heard her moving around in the room. I sat awake and saw her seated silently in the rocking chair above me. In her left hand was a flashlight. Her other hand was open and she was leaning forward and shining the light straight at her open palm. I asked her what she was looking at and slowly, as if whatever she held might feather away if she moved too fast, she held her palm out at me.

"A star," she said.

"Where?"

"I found it outside."

"Let me see."

"It's right there."

She pointed. In her palm I saw a pitch black sphere smaller than a sand grain and perfectly smooth.

"Don't touch it," she said.

"Is it alive?"

"It's heavy."

"It looks dead."

"I don't know."

"I think it needs water," I said.

She stood and walked with the star to the kitchen. I heard the water running light from the faucet.

I felt too long and tired to go after her. Leaning back on the floor I felt sleep watering over me and then I was swimming awake in a calm dark sea. I was out too far. Behind and ahead the horizon was a straight line that circled me for miles from there to there. In ten miles if the math was right a round earth would have sloped down sixty-six feet from where I was. Instead of a horizontal line I would have seen the horizon gradually sloping down from me like a hill. Without desire I drifted a long time along with the waves, watching the stars disappear and the sun hill up from under the horizon. After the morning lifted the clouds fell dark and a dense mist fogged down around me from on high. *Help.* A voice was screaming for help. Her voice: she was calling for me from somewhere too far to make out in the mist. I swam after the sound of her screaming. But she wasn't drowning when I saw her. She stood waist-deep in the flat water. As soon as she saw me a current began to loop me in concentric circles that pooled faster and faster to the center where she stood reaching her hands out for me to hold on to her. She kept screaming it. *Help.* I forgot how I knew she was going to drown me as soon as I reached the center of the smallest circle. What I remembered most purely was that even as she pushed my face underwater and pressed me downward under her palm she continued screaming for help. She was standing on a mountain of drowned bodies.

I breathed awake in the living room.

Through the window above me I watched the garden still in the morning light. The distance that light would travel in the next year was equal to six thousand billion miles.

I went to the kitchen for a glass of water. In the shards of glass at the bottom of the trash bin was the letter Marie had ripped out from her notebook. She had crunched the page into a paper ball I picked out from the glass and flattened on the surface of the floor to read:

I've been thinking over what you said and I have decided that you are right. The more I think about heaven, the more intolerable it seems. Even if we find each other there (and that seems hard enough) we will never be able to replicate the love that we have here. I do not want either of us to live without the boundaries of flesh. I do not want to just be souls, floating freely. Still, we must admit that our bodies are eventually going to wear out. Hell is not an option. So I would like to suggest a compromise. I suggest that whichever one of us dies first waits at the gates of Paradise until the other one arrives. Don't go in! After our reunion (think of it!) we'll go directly to God and request that He PLEASE put us back on earth immediately, preferably in our old bodies, but we'll take what we can get. I have no doubt He will grant this request, provided that we remember to

And there her letter ended. Every time. I pocketed the page and walked down the hall to the bedroom.

In the bed Marie was still awake. She was facing the television on the dresser and watching a show I had seen before about near-death experiences. I stood in the doorway for a few minutes listening to the narrator describe the strange case of the clinically dead blind woman who went out of her body and floated to a room on another floor of the hospital in which a husband was speaking with his sick wife. When the blind woman was resuscitated she accurately described the appearance of the husband and wife, including in her description the color of their clothes.

"Maybe this is a dream," I said.

"It's a long dream."

"But still," I said.

"Dreams have their own histories," she said.

I lay down next to her on the bed.

Not all near-death experiences were pleasant or comforting. One man drifted past the stars to a dark and endless void where demonic voices told him he was going to remain alone and conscious for the rest of time. When he woke up he never wanted to die again.

"That's right," said Marie. "You *are* dreaming."

"That's what I thought."

"You're in a coma right now."

"I know. I can't remember why."

"You almost drowned," she said.

"In the ocean," I said.

"Right," she said. "I rescued you."

"Then why am I still in a coma?"

"I was too late," she said. "You're in a hospital bed now. I see it. Hooked up to a huge beeping machine that tracks your heartbeat. And I'm sitting next to you. Holding your hand and praying for you to wake up. I've been praying for months and this is the first breakthrough. This is the part where you figure out you're dreaming. In real life your eyelids are blinking open." She turned the television off and turned back. "You believe me?"

"I think so," I said.

"You want to wake up?"

"Sure," I said.

"You have to really want to."

I looked at her looking at me. I had no reason not to believe I was real and she was still Marie. Nor had I reason to doubt that I was really in a coma and she was a hallucination produced by failing oxygen levels in my fading brain. But I felt the same indifference to both propositions as I felt when she asked me if I believed in ghosts or God or other people. What I believed was absolutely beside the point. What mattered was the truth. If the universe was speeding away from the center then the space between everything inside was just going to grow longer and longer.

"You still want to?"

"Okay," I said.

"You're sure?"

"You want me to?"

"*You* have to want to."

"Okay," I said. "I want to."

"Good," she said. "Then lean back."

She pushed me backward with her palm until I was flat on my back. Then she pinned my arms down between her knees on the bed and stared at me until I was still and staring back at her.

"Now here's what you're going to do," she said. "First you're going to close your eyes. No matter what happens you're going to keep your eyes closed. If you can do that long enough then you're going to find yourself somewhere. I can't tell you where. That depends. But what matters is that wherever you are you look for the light. At some point you're going to see a light blinking somewhere ahead of you. That's the portal. Once you see the portal you're on your way. You just have to let yourself go toward the light. You understand?"

"You talk like me."

"Do you under*stand*?"

"Yes," I said.

"Look for the light."

"The portal," I said.

"It might take a while."

"What happens when I go in?"

"You wake up."

"In the hospital?"

"In real life," she said.

"But what if I'm brain-dead?"

"You're not—"

"How do you know?"

"You are not your brain," she said. "Okay?"

She was better than I was at believing in her words. I had read her letter too many times before and felt the same nothing every time. Nothing was ever about to happen.

I shut my eyes and saw a squared darkness. Not darkness: late twilight over the water I sat before on the beach.

I was watching the waves go out and back. A dark mass of something living was moving in the sand about ten steps away from me. I walked closer and saw a monstrous creature washed up at the high tide line. Five long arms pointed out from the center of the creature, where a single eye as small and dark and round as the star that Marie had held in her hand seemed to watch me walk closer and lean down to look. I wasn't sure what to call it. In the sand I sometimes found horseshoe crabs and clamshells and snails and seaweed washed out from the waves—and this creature seemed to resemble none of them and all of them at the same time. It seemed composed somehow of separate parts of all of them and more of others. Each part grew into and out of another and so instead of a single proportionate thing I saw a barnacled heap of shells claws stones scales fins and flesh crashed out in the shape of a star on the sand and straining to break open. Each part strained to get away from the centered eye and the end of all this straining was that the creature remained stuck in the same place and seemed to quiver and pulse and hiss.

"I don't know what to do," I said.

"Keep your eyes closed."

"I am."

"What do you see?"

"I don't know what it is."

"You're supposed to see light."

"It's like a monster."

"Get away from it."

"It's just lying there."

"Get away," she said. "Look for the light."

A feeling passed too fast for me to name. I walked away from the creature to where the waves and sand were becoming the same. At the waterline I stood watching the evening turn to night. A single star pulsed white and black over the water and I felt the waves smoothing in and out over me as I watched. Each outgoing wave buried me deeper in the sand until I was waist-deep and could no longer move my legs out from inside the earth. Straight ahead of me the star blinked open and closed and open like an eyelid, swelling out more light each time and yet seeming to grow heavier. Inside I heard a long slow murmurous sound of something like a train lengthening out longer from the land behind me and sighing closer to where I stood deeper inside the sand. Just before the sound reached me the star broke open and flooded absolute light over the water. In the light I screamed my eyes awake and saw Marie in the same place she was before. The bedroom: the sun was up and the morning was full light outside the window. No sound could be heard. I looked from the window and back to her and for a full and flowing instant as we stared at each other from inside our still faces I forgot what she was and how I knew her. In that single instant she seemed as alien and unknowable as the creature on the beach, as singular and inexplicable and impossible to name, and though neither of us moved I sensed the space between us dividing inward and expanding. To even reach a hand out and touch her seemed to require an infinite series of tiny and exacting tasks. I would forever have to get halfway to where I was going.

"Marie," I said.

"You're not."

"Am I *you*?"

"No."

"I think I am."

"Stop," she said. "You're not."

I knew she was lying. And I knew that I had to leave. I went out from her and floated walking to the garden and through the woods toward the water. A season was passing around me outside. The path stuck with fallen leaves. At the beach the sand was banked with snow and the sea frozen still and solid and flat as earth. To the west an evening sun dipped full light at the horizon from beneath an immense bank of gray clouds. Back to her: I could have turned back still. Instead I moved forward over the ice and straight to where the sun held still ahead of me behind the horizon. I seemed to grow longer the longer I walked. In time I was at the edge of the earth. A thin plank of ice suspended over a starless sea of eyelid darkness. Still the sun was ahead of me—a single point of spinning light no larger than a fallen star and so close I could lift an arm and pinch it dead. Underfoot the ice slacked and creaked like a rotted branch as I stood reaching for the light. I was reaching still before I fell through. In the falling darkness, falling backward, I watched the flat underside of earth rise up from me fast and become nothing after I closed my eyes. Behind them was a space the size of the universe. It wasn't taking me anywhere.

MAY I NOT SEEM TO HAVE LIVED

In the autumn after my wife vanished I enrolled in an undergraduate course in Astronomy. The course met at the Eastern Campus of the Community College I had gone to before I got older. This was our first meeting. After taking attendance and explaining that tonight the class would go outside to learn where the constellations were and what they stood for, the Instructor led the line of us out of the Lecture Center and through the parking lot and onto a baseball field bordered by trees. No one spoke. We found our seats in the path between second and first and for a long time the Instructor moved around the pitcher's mound unpacking a telescope from out of a case and putting the parts together. When the telescope was one, he began his lecture. At the time I thought of the stars as clues to the whereabouts of my wife and so I listened to him very closely at first, taking notes that I have since lost, but which I seem to remember more visually—the written words—than anything else that went on that night. He began by admitting that he was not really an astronomer. His wife was. He was a carpenter, or had been. When his wife died, he said, seven years ago, he had lost the will to work anymore. There was nothing worth building. He had abandoned carpentry and returned to our town to become what he called a Destructionist. This meant quite literally that he took things apart. His plan, he said, was to deconstruct every object that he had ever built, starting with his house. But he stressed—he was at pains to stress—that taking something apart is in fact far more difficult than putting something together. The hard part, he said, was figuring out where one object ends and the other begins. You have to know where to stop. And to illustrate this point he took a pocketknife out of his coat and brought the blade to his wrist. Imagine I cut my hand off, he said, and moved the blade back and forth like the bow of a violin. And imagine now, he said, that after the wound heals I replace the old hand with a metal one. The metal hand is mine for a long time, and at some point, suspend your disbelief, I forget all about the flesh and blood that was there to begin with. I forget that I was once complete and come to believe that the metal hand is the realest and most original part of me. I come in fact to feel that not only the other hand but also the rest of the body I was born with is somehow counterfeit—somehow inconsistent with the rest of me. And so I decide to do away with it. One at a time I take away all the original parts and replace them with metal ones that match the make of the hand. I perform another operation every day and eventually I am completely metal; not a trace of flesh remains.

Now the question I want you to think about, he said, is whether I am the same person now as I was before. If not, then I want you to locate the exact instant when I was born and the previous version of me disappeared. He did not go on but lowered his eyes and looked through the telescope at whatever was in the sky. Finished, he left the lens focused downward and—I noticed this much later—directly at me. The truth, he said, walking away from the telescope, was that there was no way of telling one part from another. Change is constant. So we must conclude that in fact I was never the same person—not even before I turned to metal. I am always someone else. And this truth (he went on) was what eventually derailed his plan to become a destructionist. He had discovered one day after taking the legs off his kitchen table and placing them next to one another on the floor that to destroy anything—to truly reduce any one object into an essential and everlasting essence—is impossible. There is no essence. The table that had once been one was now something else, true. But the legs were still their own. Even if he were to saw them in two or three or four more halves he would never get to the end. Even an atom can split open. And though another mind might have taken comfort in this discovery, said the Instructor, he could not. He was terrified. He had been working at an unblinking pace for an entire summer, he said, and now as he looked around the kitchen he wondered for the first time what he had meant to accomplish. There was almost nothing left of the house that he had built in the months before his marriage—nothing except the walls and the floor and a few more pieces of furniture that he had set aside for later. The table was below him and he remembered picking up one of the legs and running the flame from a lighter along the length of the wood, thinking that he might burn the house down and breathe the smoke to death. But the fire never caught. It blackened the wood and went out when he brought the flame back. And somehow that was what had saddened the Instructor the most—the black that appeared on the wood where the fire had been. That was what he was looking at when he began to feel an enormous distance from everything, as though the earth were flattening out and away from him. To move from one place to another would take too long. He stood completely still, not letting go of the leg of the table, which seemed, he said, to become heavier and heavier in his hands, so that he felt—he remembered the fact more than the feeling—that he was sinking into the floor of the kitchen. He must have fainted. When he awoke he was lying on his back. The stars were over him and he was staring and staring at the spaces between them. The word stare, he said, comes from the Flengarian verb stareo, which means to eye with the detention of thought, or to contemplate. But stareo itself derives from another Flengarian word, starus, meaning star. Stareo starum, reads the first line of a poem by Selenus—poem number III—and scholars have argued for centuries about how to translate these words. I stare at the star, runs the conservative translation. And yet this translation ignores the potential that we might read the noun, starum, as an objective form of the verb, stareo, in which case the translation would go something like: I stare at the act of staring, or, I contemplate contemplation. The matter becomes further complicated in light of other and less literal interpretations, such as that the poet might have been writing from the perspective of the star, or that the word starus was often used during the first century after the birth of Christ (and the death of Selenus) as slang for infinity. And so we find that from one line of poetry written more than two thousand years ago a seemingly endless line of potential meanings emerge:

1. I star the star.
2. I contemplate infinity.
3. I am a star, staring at myself.
4. I can't stop staring.
5. I am infinitely stared at.
6. The star lasts as long as I stare at it.
7. I stare forever.
8. I immortalize the star.

To insist that one translation is right and the rest are wrong is of course to miss the point, said the Instructor. The point is simply that the line between what you are and what you're observing is erasable—that if you stare at an object all the way and without limitation you are no longer anything else. You're everything. That was what the Instructor had realized when he awoke on the floor of the kitchen. He realized that he was not separate from the stars. And nor (the implication was obvious) was he separate from his wife. Destroying his house had been an attempt to do away with her. He knew that now. But the truth was she had never left. The truth was he could bring her back whenever he wanted to. And not merely as metaphor or memory or photograph in his mind: More than that. More than just remembrance: He could make the memory actual and touchable and intimate as the act of prayer. He could in fact become his wife. He already was, he said. What he meant by that he went no further to explain, he refused, for he felt that his meaning planed so far ahead of words that we would be better off (if we really hoped to understand) forgetting everything he had told us and starting over from square one. Forget I'm even here, he said. Forget that you're here. Just stare at the stars and imagine that the line between the two of you—the line that conveys the train of your thoughts—is straight and infinite and indestructible. You're that line, said the Instructor. In the silence that went after this assignment I watched the Instructor peer through the telescope and a number of students walk away from the field and disappear forever into the forest. I watched the few that were left gaze at the stars with expressions that must have reminded me—I remember writing the comparison in my notes, though I can no longer summon the visual image of anyone in that class—of a painting called The Gates of Paradise, a print of which my wife had taped to the wall of our bedroom, and which displayed a small black circle, about the size of an eyeball, at the center of an oversized and otherwise completely blank canvas. I tried to look along but nothing was there. Nothing was a fact I found wherever I looked. Perhaps that was the point. But I had thought the same word before—I had thought: Nothing—and no matter how many times I multiplied and translated and twisted after the end of this thought, I always arrived at the same locked door, the same anxious sense of idling and needing to do something fast—to go swimming or plant a tree or build a house or learn another language so thoroughly that I forgot how to speak the one I was born with. And I couldn't do that now. I was supposed to sit still. That was what my wife would have wanted, I kept telling myself, and this refrain convinced me, if not to commune with the stars, then at least to stare at them, and more importantly, to stare at everyone else, and to search their faces for evidence of sincerity, of an authentic connection with something immortal and timeless and unconditional. I didn't find it. Most of the students just looked bored; the rest were trying too hard. I felt, watching them, the way I remember feeling in church after the body of Christ was passed out and everyone knelt at the pews and prayed. Not envy. I never wanted to talk to God directly. What the worshipers were thinking about never interested me. I was interested in what God was thinking, and though the concept of prayer—or anyway, of applying the name *prayer* to a certain sequence of thoughts, and presuming that the rest of our thoughts are something other than and separate from prayers—always struck me as innately and self-evidently absurd, I believed, as I looked around the church, as a child, and now, as I looked around the baseball field, that God was listening to each of us, closely, and that He was horrified. He was thinking: Stop! You're going about this all wrong! He was—at least, I believed that He was—an unceasingly sad animal, God, and His sadness, I thought, was rooted in an escalating sense of physical and emotional exhaustion, an awareness that the race of humans, which He had intended to one day become His helpers, and perhaps His partners in the profession of supervising the universe, would never learn to leave Him alone, never stop asking Him to explain and justify and adjudicate their presence on earth, and that, worst of all, He could not abandon or even blame us for acting the way we did. He was at fault. He was our father. In this regard, I realized, and I wrote this realization in my notes, thinking that I had, at last, found an important clue, God reminded me somewhat of my wife, whose frequent complaints that I wasn't what she wanted, that I was selfish, that I was always asking and never giving, were invariably followed by periods of profound repentance, during which, after retiring to her bedroom, and locking the door, so that I had to go outside and climb through the window in order to get back to her, she apologized over and over, and assured me that she was wrong, she was selfish, she should stop trying to change me into something I wasn't. She loved me. She did. And yet, she said, she only wished that I would empathize with her once in a while, really empathize, rather than just thinking the word empathy and claiming it for myself. She wanted to know that I was part of her, that when she felt sad, for instance, I did too, and that our sadness was something we bore together and at the same time. And since this was what I had always thought God wanted, since God's greatest hope, I thought, was for someone to feel what He felt, to share the awful responsibility of omniscience, I understood, sitting in the field, that the act of love was not so far removed from that of religious faith, and I even scribbled, on a separate page of my notes, and in letters large enough that the Instructor—who had, without my noticing, walked to where I was sitting, and was standing right in front of me—must have been able to make them out, an equation that I no longer consider complete:

$$|E_g| \approx \frac{GM}{R} = E_k \approx \frac{M^{2/3}N^{5/3}\hbar^2}{2mR^2}.$$

The Instructor said nothing direct about this equation. But the long way he looked at me after I had closed the notebook suggested that he had seen what I had written and that he thought I was on to something. Have you read Genesis, he asked. I had. Then you must know, he said, that whereas Eve eats the fruit out of kindness, because she doesn't want to disappoint the serpent, Adam's sin is that he loves his wife more than God. Adam eats the fruit out of fear that when Eve leaves, he will be totally alone. Without her, he thinks, said the Instructor, even Eden seems unbearable. He stared at me. His stare was softer than that of the students at the stars, and staring back at him, I began to sense that the space between us was no longer there, and that he was reading the words that were passing through my mind. Probably this was paranoia. I realize that. But the thought that he might indeed know what I was thinking struck me at the time as so disturbing that without deciding to I began thinking the word *no* over and over again, so that there was nothing else for him to hear. After another moment he returned to the pitcher's mound and resumed his lecture, pointing out the constellations with the blade of the pocketknife. As I reclined in the grass, watching this man, and wondering whether I knew him, and from where, I began to lose consciousness, and this sense of slowness, of *dreamulous languor*, as the phrase appeared to me at the time, endured for the duration of the lecture, despite my efforts to come out of it. I still remember the weight of my thoughts—the gravity—as I gazed up at that sky, at Carina, Cassiopeia, Kepler, Hydrus, Infiniti, Microscopium, and more, more constellations until at last, unable to tell one figure from the next, and starting to suspect that the Instructor was no longer naming actual patterns, but simply inventing new ones as he went along, I gave up listening and let my eyes close, waiting for sleep to pass through me. Even as the lecture drew to an end I remained in this position, prostrate, hearing as if from inside another room my classmates gathering up and into the silence, apparently having forgotten all about my existence, as I had in some sense forgotten myself. Yet I was not completely asleep— not yet. I had the weird sensation of watching the world through my eyelids, and what I saw after the class was dismissed was the Instructor standing at the pitcher's mound and training the telescope directly at my face, which he studied closely, pausing at times to jot notes in the margins of a large book that I believed to be a dictionary. It was some time before I waked. The grass was wet and the sight of the fog hovering over the field, so thick that I could no longer make out the outline of the outfield fence, convinced me for the spasm of several seconds that I was perhaps in heaven—a conviction that grew stronger when I remembered the dream I had just come up from under. In the dream I had been sitting alone inside a small railroad coach that was stationed along a narrow track. After embarking from under the backstop of the baseball field, the train had accelerated through the forest and out across the plains, past farm after farm of corn and cows and wheat and wildflowers, traveling at the astonishing speed of something between sound and sight toward the end of an earth that I believed, as some of the sailors on the Santa Maria are said to have believed, despite copious evidence to the contrary, and despite the repeated assurances of Columbus, to be flat, and more to the point, finite. *Stop the train*, I shouted, shutting my eyes, and fearing that at any moment we might tumble headlong over the edge of the universe. But I could not make myself understood, and when at last I opened my eyes I saw that I was sitting across from a man I recognized as the reincarnation of the astronomer Nicholaus Copernicus, whose *De revolutionibus orbium coelestium*, published in 1543, was the first written proposal of the heretical hypothesis that the universe was without a center. Your wife has gone a long way off, said the man, shaking his head. Tonight she's really gone a long way, he said, and it's no use looking for her anymore. And everyone, he went on after a long while, looking out the window at the lines of starlight, is your wife. Everyone you talk to, everyone you ride with and look at stars with is someone you used to love. You must, he said, have learned some astronomy in school. You know that the earth isn't the center of the universe. Everyone accepts that without question now because the scientists proved it. But in the old days the church said the earth was the center, and there were constant debates about which side was correct. Just as everyone who ever lived, said Copernicus, believes their god is the true God. But what we do to the ones who believe in different gods is enough to make us doubt ourselves. Then we argue about whether we're apes or fallen angels, and no one can clearly define the difference between the two. But if we look very closely, and if we learn how to separate the true beliefs from the false ones, then perhaps, he said, faith can become synonymous with science. At this point Copernicus lowered his head and, praying, pronounced what I later learned were the last words of another famous stargazer, Tycho Brahe, whose death, according to the report written by his doctor, Johann Jessensius Jessen, was occasioned by the bursting of his bladder, eleven days after a banquet with the Bohemian Count of Rosenberg, during which the astronomer had been too courteous to get up and go to the bathroom. Brahe's Assistant, Johannes Kepler, who in 1596, at the age of 24, had published the first and most forceful defense of the Copernican model, and whose reputation would eventually eclipse that of his mentor, observed Brahe's long and unspeakably painful descent into delirium, and recorded at sometime between nine and ten in the morning of October 24, 1601, his dying sentence, which we can only assume was addressed to God, and which was spoken, according to Kepler, in a state of feverish and dreamlike anguish:

Ne frusta vixisse vidar.

May I not seem to have lived in vain, was how I translated this sentence, and what struck me even in sleep, and even more so when I waked, was the indecision implicit in the word *seem*—as though after years of patient and contemplative research, Brahe was less certain than ever about what was happening to him and even whether he had lived at all. After repeating this phrase several times, Brahe had closed his eyes and let go of life peacefully, having realized, Kepler writes, that death is nothing more than another dream, and that everyone is always someone else. And indeed, it was not until I had come to a similar conclusion and resigned myself to the fate of falling endlessly and effortlessly through the indefinite expanse of space and time that the train slowed to a stop, opening its doors on a vast green field which the waking Copernicus, waving his arms, claimed to be the Kingdom of Christ, the Kingdom of Christ! This was the last moment of the dream that I could recall, and the memory merged with what I was looking at now. The students were gone. There were few stars left. The only factual evidence corroborating the night before was the telescope, which the Instructor had left standing on the pitcher's mound, and the notebook, which had somehow traveled out of my pocket and lay open on the ground beneath the telescope. How this had happened I had no clue. But I would not have been surprised to learn that I was responsible. What I remember most unimpeachably is the sense of loss that overcame me in the moment after I walked to the mound and turned the notebook to the page the equation was on.

$$|E_g| \approx \frac{GM}{R} = E_k \approx \frac{M^{2/3}N^{5/3}\hbar^2}{2mR^2}.$$

I no longer understood it! Whatever revelation I had been about to uncover had dissolved, as dreams will, and what remained on the page appeared (and still appears, despite the fact that I can decipher the symbols, and that I can precisely recall the sequence of thoughts that led me to compose them) completely nonsensical. Pocketing the notebook, I walked to the mound and trained the telescope at the night. Through the eyepiece I saw something in outer space—something between two of the stars and brighter than both of them, completely still. At first it was nothing more than a point of light:

•

But as I watched the light began to elongate. Soon the original point was the end—or the start—of a line that stretched for what must have been more than a million light years across the dome of the Milky Way.

———————————

The line grew several minutes longer before the back end began, gradually, to go forward, following after the front, which was, I noticed, no longer moving. Someone was erasing the line—that was what it looked like from where I stood. I watched. But I never felt that I was watching something disappear. I felt instead as though the light was turning away from me and moving over the horizon. Not ending—just entering another dimension. Deeper. Now there was nothing but a single point on the other side of space.

•

This point grew progressively smaller. Not until the light had vanished completely did I step back from the telescope and remember where I was. The fog had lifted. The earth was flat. I heard the birds in the branches and the distant sound of a train getting longer and longer and longer.

PROPORTIONS
FOR THE HUMAN FIGURE

In the morning before she died Marie slept late. I had
eaten breakfast and was sitting at the kitchen table
reading a book about the self when she came in wearing
her nightgown and holding an ashtray I had used to light
a stick of incense the night before. I asked if she had gone
to the bathroom. She told me she had gone and so I sat
her down at the table and set a grapefruit and a bowl of
oatmeal with raisins on the placemat in front of her. I
watched her work the pits out into the ashtray on the placemat. She winced when she spooned the first grapefruit
section into her mouth. But her hunger was there and she
ate most of her breakfast without talking about the past. I
looked out the window. I was out of sorts because the deer
had made a third attack on the vegetable plants. A single
bird perched at the birdhouse that hung from the maple.
Not eating—just considering the seeds inside the circular
hole. The bird flew down from the birdhouse and beaked

106

after the worms in the earth. Marie looked through the window at the grown-over garden.

"Who is Samuel to me?" she asked.

"He's your son."

"But he never calls me Mom."

"Yes he does."

"I knew him first," she said.

"You were there when he was born."

She ate her oatmeal. I went back to the book about the self. The author was describing an experiment in which people were asked to swallow their own saliva. No one had a problem with that. But then the same people were asked to spit into a sparkling clean drinking glass and drink their own spit. Most of them were repulsed and refused to drink from the glass without the promise of a monetary reward. On the basis of this experiment the author concluded that the self was a phenomenal entity located somewhere inside the human body. That which leaves the body is no longer part of the self.

I closed the book. Marie circled her spoon around the eaten inside of the grapefruit. Then she stood and went to her room where her ointment and elastic stockings were laid out. I followed and she sat at the end of the unmade bed and stared at the floor.

"Give me your leg," I said.

"This one?"

"*Your* leg."

I pointed at the scars above her knees and asked if she remembered having blisters there.

"When was that?"

"Last week," I said.

I spread cortisone ointment on her legs. She dressed

herself and went to the living room where I sat her down in her reclining chair and covered her body with the wool blanket she liked.

"Do you want to watch the Mass?"

"No," she said. "But only if you do."

"That's not a good reason."

I turned the television on and watched the mass. The priest was a missionary from somewhere else and his sermon was about the afterlife. He said that heaven was the working out of a great love affair. As each celestial day passes the inhabitants of heaven come to love one another more fully. Human love grows and grows and God grows along with our love. He gets fatter.

"How long is that going to be on?"

"Forever," I said. "Do you want to take a nap?"

I muted the television and let her sleep. When the Mass was over I went out to the garden and dug up hosta lilies around the birdhouse and picked some tomatoes for salad. Walking back to the house I watched the cat have a confrontation with a deer. The cat was urinating under a tree and the deer walked over to him and stomped its foot a few times until the cat ran away. He ran inside after me and leapt onto the arm of the chair Marie slept in. I sat down next to her and closed my eyes. I was still thinking about the sermon—about God growing fatter and fatter.

In the space before I fell asleep I remembered a story I had read as a child about a tree that wanted to find out where the food chain ceased. The tree was a master of meditation and so was able to attain a state of concentration in which he could depart from his flesh and communicate with all the other creatures in the forest. First he asked the worms. "We don't know," they answered, "but surely the birds will know. Go and ask them." The birds could not answer his question either and directed him to the rabbits and the rabbits in turn directed him to the foxes. No one knew. The foxes directed him to the wolves, the wolves referred him to the lions, the lions pointed him to the humans, and the humans led him back to the worms. Finally the tree approached the Sun, who answered: "I am the sun, mighty, unconquerable, creator, all-seeing, all-knowing, master, maker of light, giver of life." The tree was puzzled. Again he asked where the food chain ceased and again the sun gave the same response. "Sun," said the tree, "That is not what I asked you." At that point the sun darkened and took the tree aside. "The animals on earth think I know everything," said the sun, "so I can't speak in their presence. The truth is I don't know where the food chain ends. You had better go to heaven and put your question to God."

When I awoke Marie was gone. I heard the water running in the bathroom and went to look for her.

"I've forgotten what to do with this," she said.

She was standing in the mirror holding a toothbrush with toothpaste on it. I gave her the electric toothbrush. "Yes," she said. "That's what I wanted." She turned on the electric toothbrush and held the end in one hand while brushing her teeth with the first toothbrush. I took the first one away from her. "Use *this* one," I said, and she brushed her teeth for the full two minutes that the electric toothbrush was programmed for. After she was finished I saw that I had forgotten to put toothpaste on it.

"Go to the kitchen," I said, "and I'll get your pills."

"What pills?"

"Your numbers," I said. "Go on, you gutter lily you."

In the kitchen she sat and looked at the newspaper. On the page she opened to was a picture of a group of people holding signs in a sunlit field. She asked what they were doing and I told her they were protesting a plan to build an enormous telescope on the top of a sacred mountain.

"What's a telescope?"

"It's a device for seeing things in space."

"What do they see, stars?"

"Yes, that and more."

She looked at the picture. I brought her a bowl filled with ice cubes. After she drank her pills I turned the television back on and switched the channels around and around.

I stopped at a program about the origin of the universe. An astronomer stood at a blackboard talking about quasars. The power of a quasar depends on the amount of matter that the black hole at the center consumes. Since black holes are big eaters and consume the equivalent of several suns each year, quasars are the most luminous objects in the known universe.

Marie dipped her hand into the bowl and retrieved an ice cube. She put the cube in her mouth.

"Have you ever had any impure thoughts?" I asked.

"No, I don't think so."

She took another ice cube from the bowl on the table in front of her. Her eyes were on her palm, which cupped the cube like a caught moth. The ice melted to water and the water leaked through her fingers until her palm held nothing. That was how time passed.

"We're not really married," I said.

"Then I can do whatever I want."

I turned back to the television. The astronomer drew a

circle on the blackboard. Inside the circle he wrote *Black Hole*. The border of the black hole was called the accretion disk. Particles of matter spiral into this disk like water down a drain, spinning faster and faster, and compressing. Most of the matter ends up sucked in. But some of the particles—he drew an arrow pointing out of the circle and stretching almost to the end of the blackboard—are regurgitated in the form of gaseous jets that speed away from the accretion disk and extend thousands of light years across space-time. Nobody knows what causes the black hole to swallow certain particles and spit others out.

Marie walked to the closet. She opened the door and took out the shoebox full of mementos from different phases of our marriage. She turned the box upside down on the table. Papers and photos slid out. She ignored the photos and sifted through the papers. I asked her what she was looking for. "The circle," she said. But she meant the ring that I had fashioned from a sterling silver spoon and given to her as a gift for her seventy-seventh birthday. I knew because she had lost this ring several times in the past few months. The last time I had found it over the lid of a perfume bottle in the medicine cabinet.

"It's not in there," I said.

She ignored me. I turned the television off and walked to the table to help her look.

I picked up an envelope without an address. Inside it was a story Marie had written many years ago about a turtle that lived alone in a forest in the time before Eden. Even after exploring this forest for hundreds of years the turtle had not once encountered another living creature. His solitude was not however a source of sadness—not at first. Except in the mornings, when he sometimes longed to tell the trees about his dreams, he hardly ever noticed that he was alone, and this longing to communicate with something other than his own mind dimmed the moment he emerged from his shell and began moving around in search of his next meal. More even than eating, the turtle loved tasting food, and since he took care never to eat too much, his hunger was never quite satiated, and he always had something else to search for.

And then one morning he looked up from a blackberry bush and sighted a hawk—he knew the name instantly: *hawk*—gliding hard above the trees and heading in the direction where the sun went down. So fast was the flight of this hawk that he was gone before the turtle had a chance to call out to him. Hours passed. The turtle stood motionless, hoping that the hawk might return, eating nothing, and repeating the same word over and over again: *Hawk! Hawk!* But the sky remained vacant, and when finally the sun fell under the earth he went back inside his shell and contemplated the word *sleep*. That night he had a long nightmare in which the hawk heard him screaming and circled down landing next to him. In the nightmare the turtle asked if there were any other animals in the forest. The hawk looked around for a few seconds as if making sure he was in the right place. "No," he said. "I think you're the only one here."

I folded the page back into the envelope before I reached the end of the story.

Marie was holding a thin square of paper.

"Are you an animal?" I asked.

"I don't know."

"An angel?"

"Maybe," she said.

"Do you love me?"

"It's possible."

I looked more closely at the paper in her hand. A receipt: it proved that in the summer we moved here she had purchased a shovel from the hardware store down the street. I remembered that she had brought the shovel back home and immediately set about digging a deep hole in the garden. She dug until the top of the hole was higher than she was and the water at the bottom was up to her knees. Then I heard her calling for me. "I'm stuck," she said when I found her. I brought the ladder from the shed and after she climbed out we sat alongside the hole for a while and talked about how deep it was. An earthworm lengthened out from the soil drifted around us. It wasn't all the way out when she pinched the end between her fingers and pulled the rest of the worm into space. She asked me if I knew which end was the head. "Neither," I said. The end she wasn't holding swept back and forth. At no point did we decide to, but she put the earthworm down on the soil and I sliced it in half with the point of the shovel. One half went into the shape of a boomerang. The other never moved again. The hole became a mulch pit in the garden behind the line of apple trees she planted a few months later. Earthworms can live up to eight years.

She picked up a pen. Her hand steadied long enough to draw a circle on a page of lined paper.

"Write down orangutan for me," she said.

"Why?"

"So I can have it."

I sat next to her. I wrote RANGUTAN after the circle and then passed the pen back to her.

"Draw a bird," I said.

"No."

"A star?"

"No. I can't."

I took the pen back from her. Around ORANGUTAN I drew flying birds—two joined parenthesis on their sides—and five-pointed stars—up, down, up, across, and down—and a moon almost full. I drew grass at the bottom of the page and standing upright on the grass I drew an orangutan with his arms stretched out like Christ. Marie looked out the window. She asked if I saw the squirrel that had climbed up to the birdhouse and was pawing after the seeds inside. I said yes without looking up because I was drawing a tree and the squirrel was there all the time. Inside of the O that began ORANGUTAN I drew a black hole. It looked like the funnel of an eyeball. I shaped the T into a crucifix before I gave the card to Marie.

"Write it down for me," she said.

"What?"

"You know."

"Papa Cup?"

"Yes," she said. "Write it down because I can't."

Marie had told me once about a scientist who had tried to train an orangutan to speak like a person. The orangutan had learned to pronounce two words—*papa* and *cup*. Then he got sick from a high fever. On his deathbed the orangutan held the scientist's hand and repeated the words *papa cup* over and over again for several hours until he lost consciousness and died. She still remembered this story and asked me sometimes why I had laughed the first time she told it. I wasn't sure.

I wrote PAPA CUP in a bubble pointed at the open mouth of the orangutan and passed the page back to her.

She read the words without reacting to them.

I went to the stove and heated the pot of soup left over from last night. Marie looked out the window at the garden. Night was promised. Still the chance persisted that the sun might not rise tomorrow morning.

The soup looked done. I was ladling it into a bowl when I heard Marie calling me to come see "the poor creature" in the backyard. She pointed out the window. A box turtle was standing still in the weeds next to the tomato plants.

I went outside and picked the turtle up from the base of his shell and he pushed his head all the way out to see what I was. His eyes were red. His feet swam forward at the air before flattening back inside his shell. I brought him into the house and placed him at the bottom of the empty box on the table. She sat and leaned closer to look at him.

"Is that Harry?" she asked.

Harry was a box turtle who lived in our garden for many years. He had been injured a few summers ago when I ran into him with a power mower. Though I pulled the mower back before the blades could tear him up a crack appeared along the side of his shell. Marie repaired the crack with glue and fed him berries and insects for the next few weeks. He survived that summer and after he had stopped eating I found a good place for him to hibernate in the stump of an elm tree that had fallen down during Hurricane Diana. I thought he wanted me to. I had read somewhere that turtles that forget to hibernate endure a progressive physical and mental decline and eventually become sterile. But that February as I was burning fallen branches in the backyard I found Harry crawling out of the fire with smoke coming out from under his back. He must have moved. I buried him in the damp earth of the garden to cool him off. Marie found him there a few weeks later, his legs outstretched as if he was trying to shed his burning shell.

"No," I said. "Harry went to the other side."

The turtle was still hiding. She leaned forward to look at his shell. Without looking away she lifted the spoon from the soup I had left on the placemat in front of her, spilling some of it on the picture of the orangutan. I paper-toweled the soup off the picture and watched her tap the round end of the spoon against the shell of the turtle. "He's stuck," she said. I took the turtle away from her and moved the box out of her reach.

"Eat," I said.

"I can't."

"Try."

"You try."

She watched the steam rise vanishing from the bowl. I sat next to her and spooned some soup into my mouth.

"Eating is what it's all about," I said. "One animal feeds on another. Satan roams the earth devouring humans. And humans eat the flesh of Christ. We drink his blood in the Eucharist."

I lifted the spoon at her. She swallowed the first spoonful without looking at me. After that she kept hanging her head and turning away from me. I didn't force her to eat because the hospice staff had told me that food and drink caused distress if the body was trying to shut down. But I still felt like I was starving her. She was staring at me. The inside of the house was beginning to grow dark and in the few lines of sunlight that bent through the windows I thought I saw a look of understanding in her eyes.

"I want to go home," she said.

"You are home."

"No."

"You've lived with me for almost sixty years. Your home is here."

She was crying. I turned the lights on. Often rather than comforting her I needed only to increase the amount of light in the room around her and her mood would lift. I thought sometimes that if I studied this phenomenon I might learn something new about the afterlife. I remembered the television priest asking us to imagine God as a single point of light that overflows its source and moves in concentric circles to the ends of the heavenly universe. He said that at the outer periphery of the circles the light begins to fade. Not because God lacks power to expand that far, but because the people at the periphery are poor conductors. There it remains dark and cold.

"Is home on earth?" I asked.

"Yes."

"But your mother and father are in heaven. Is that where you want to go?"

"Yes," she said. "But it has been a long time, and I don't know when this is going to end."

I always knew when she had to go to the bathroom because she rocked back and forth in her seat. She was rocking fast and her hands formed into fists before I helped her out of her chair and walked her to the toilet. She told me to go away when I sat her down.

I went out into the hall and stood at the door listening for the flush. After an interval of silence I heard water running light out of the faucet. The water ran longer and longer and I opened the door to see if she was all right.

She wasn't washing her hands. She was just standing at the sink watching the water whirlpool down into the drain.

"You don't have to be in here now," she said.

I closed the door and went back to the breakfast table. A moth hovered over the lentils and angled away when I closed in.

In the box the turtle was stretching his head aloft to look over the wall. His neck wasn't long enough. It would only make her sadder. I brought him outside with the bowl of soup and set him down in the garden where I had found him. He was already pushing away from me when his feet touched the earth. The weeds curtained after him when he went through. He felt no hunger for food. His only hunger was to find the hawk from his nightmare. He remembered that in the moment before he awakened the hawk had consented to fly him to another forest where all the other animals lived. But he couldn't remember which direction that was and so he decided to just walk toward the sun. In the evenings he walked west and in the mornings he walked east. And because his eyes were always on the heavens he never realized that he was walking back and forth along the same path of earth.

I walked to the garden with the soup and dumped it in the mulch pile at the bottom of the hole. Eighteen hundred miles below was the molten core of earth, spinning faster than the surface. I was thinking about the afterlife. A flock of black birds—Marie might have been able to name what kind—had landed in the branches of the trees that bordered the backyard and were talking to one another about where to go next. In heaven I will ask her to walk to the outer rims with me. The center is so bright that no creature can remain long in its presence.

I threw the bowl into the trees and the birds flocked out from the branches and south for the winter.

Inside the house was still and darkening. Marie sat on the sofa holding a stack of photographs. "Of the old days," she said when I sat next to her. I took the stack from her and she rested her head on my shoulder as we looked through the photos. Perhaps our guardian angels were collaborating. She hadn't shown that much affection in a long time. She pointed at a picture of me standing in front of the ocean with my arms stretched out and my legs straight. The sun was setting behind me, and framed against the horizon, I appeared as nothing more than a dark and distant figure of perfectly human proportions.

"I wish you still looked like that," she said.

"Like what?"

"Light."

"I am light."

I let go of her hand and walked to the window. I stood in front of the evening spreading my arms out as I had in the photograph.

"Look at you," she said. "You walk around with your shirt unbuttoned and your stomach falling out. I used to be able to carry you around in my hands."

She turned back to the picture. I closed my eyes and stood in the same position feeling my arms grow heavier and heavier.

I remembered reading once about a woman named Mrs. White who was said to have held a forty pound Bible in the palm of her outstretched hand for over half an hour one evening at a gathering of the faithful in the autumn of 1822. Her other hand turned the pages of the Bible and pointed at passages that she quoted word for word without looking at them. Mrs. White was a founder of the Adventist church and her followers viewed this episode as proof that she was a prophet.

I don't know how long I stood there with my arms out. I must have outdistanced Mrs. White. When I opened my eyes the lights were off and the room was dark. After a few seconds my vision deepened enough to make out Marie sleeping in the chair with her head leaned back and the photos fallen on the floor around her. A gurgling sound was coming from her open mouth. I flicked the light switch on the wall behind me. It didn't come on. The lamp on the fan wasn't working either and so I lit one of her candles and placed it on the table. I later learned that our neighbor had crashed his car into the telephone pole down the street and taken our electricity out. He was swerving to avoid an animal.

I took her wrist. The pulse was there. But her breathing was irregular and there was a long space when I heard no breathing at all. After that the gurgling began again, weaker this time. I gathered the photographs from the floor into the box with the papers and pictures and receipts and whatever else we saved for some reason. Not looking at them hurt. I put the box in the closet for good. The drawing I left open on the table with the orangutan watching her sleep. His larynx was too high. Otherwise he might have said more than *Papa Cup*. He might have asked what the difference was.

The book about the self was open in front of me. I picked it up and read the last page. Perhaps there exists a part of the human body that persists intact from the moment of conception to the moment of death. That was what the author hypothesized. He located this immutable part deep inside the brain. It was too small for the scientists to ever find. Its sole function was to remain the same as the rest of the self changed.

I closed the book and looked at Marie. Her name was still Marie. To imagine her as a heap of ashes and a few bone fragments was horrifying. But she didn't want to be buried in the earth where the worms would eat her.

In the darkness I reached out for her. I found her hand and she held on to me without moving anything else. Then the rest of her awakened and she sat for a certain length of eternity looking along the walls and out the window and at the candle and the picture on the table for some connection between now and then. And then she saw me. Her eyes remembered me. She said that she had a good dream that there were a lot of people around and everyone loved her. I wasn't there.